A TRUE PRINCESS

DIANE ZAHLER

A TRUE PRINCESS

HARPER

An Imprint of HarperCollinsPublishers

Library of Congress Cataloging-in-Publication Data
Zahler, Diane.
A true princess / Diane Zahler. — 1st ed.
    p. cm.
Summary: Twelve-year-old Lilia goes north to seek the family she has never
known, accompanied by her friends Kai and Karina and their dog Ove, on an
adventure fraught with peril, especially when they become lost in Bitra Forest,
the Elf King's domain. Inspired by the Hans Christian Andersen tale, The
princess and the pea.
ISBN 978-0-06-182501-9 (trade bdg.)
[1. Fairy tales. 2. Identity—Fiction. 3. Princesses—Fiction. 4. Voyages
and travels—Fiction. 5. Heroism—Fiction. 6. Lost children—Fiction.
7. Friendship—Fiction.] I. Title.
PZ8.Z17Tru 2011   2010017846
[Fic]—dc22   CIP
                                                                               AC

Frontispiece illustration by Yvonne Gilbert
Typography by Joel Tippie
11 12 13 14 15 LP/RRDB 10 9 8 7 6 5 4 3 2 1
❖

First Edition

For Ben, the real Prince Tycho

My deepest gratitude to:

Barbara Lalicki and Maria Gomez, for their diligence, patience, and skill

Shani Soloff, for her tireless readings and inspired suggestions

Debra and Arnie Cardillo, for their encouragement and support

Kathy Zahler, for listening, reading, and cheering

*And Phil Sicker, who is not least but most—most constant reader,
most exceptional editor, most devoted husband*

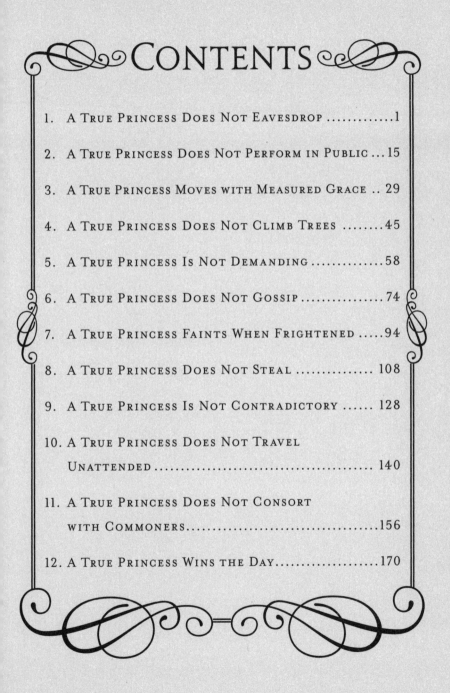

CONTENTS

1

A TRUE PRINCESS
DOES NOT EAVESDROP

I shall run away!" I whispered furiously to Ove the sheepdog as we crouched beneath the farmhouse window listening to the conversation inside. I could hardly believe what I was hearing.

"I meant what I said," I heard Ylva say to her husband, Jorgen. "Lilia will have to go. I have spoken to Odur the miller. He and his wife have need of a serving girl, and they would be pleased to take her."

Lilia. The sound of my name on her lips horrified me. I covered my mouth so I wouldn't make any noise, though I wanted to scream. The miller was a burly man with a rough manner and rougher hands. He had six children and he beat them all, and I knew he would strike a servant even more frequently.

"We have no room for one more," Ylva continued. "Would you prefer to give Odur one of your own children?" I raised my head just enough to peer through the window and saw Jorgen smoking his last pipe of the day before the fire. Ylva, newly pregnant, sat beside him in the rocking chair.

Jorgen cleared his throat and replied mildly, "I know that my children are not yours, my dear, and that our own baby will have first place in your heart. But I love them. I cannot send Kai or Karina away."

"Of course you cannot, husband," Ylva said in an oily tone. "But Lilia is almost thirteen, and old enough to make her own way in the world."

"I do not think Lilia would want to be the miller's servant," Jorgen pointed out.

"I am not asking you," Ylva retorted. "She has taken advantage of us long enough. These ten years and more we have fed her and clothed her, and she has been as useless to us as a barren ewe. It is time for her to go."

"Now, wife—," Jorgen said calmly.

She turned on him ferociously, and I stooped lower so that she would not see me through the window. "Do you want this babe I am carrying to go without? How shall we feed him, with Lilia eating us out of house and home?"

"She does not eat so much," Jorgen protested. "And she could help care for the baby."

"Karina will do that," Ylva said to him. "She can take over Lilia's indoor duties as well, and Kai can surely mind the sheep alone. We have no need for Lilia. And besides, the miller has offered to pay us in coppers and to give us as much flour as we might need for next winter."

Jorgen sighed deeply. He knew, as I did, that when Ylva's mind was set on something, there was no changing it. She had once made Jorgen walk miles from Hagi, the village nearest where we lived, to Brenna Town because she longed for strawberries and there were none at our market. What she wanted she got. I would have to go; that was clear. But I swore to myself that I would not go to the miller. I would not be sold like a slave for a few pounds of flour!

I sat beneath the window, stroking Ove and trembling with rage and dread as I heard Jorgen and Ylva climb the ladder to the sleeping loft, where Kai and Karina already slept. I knew now that the old saying "Eavesdroppers seldom hear anything good about themselves" was true.

I repeated the conversation over and over in my mind. Ylva was right when she said that I was a useless servant. I did daydream often, and I forgot to do half the things she demanded, or I did them poorly. I was never comfortable enough on a bed, nor a cot or pallet, to sleep well at night, so I often dozed off over the washing-up or fell into a dream in the middle of sweeping. I cooked porridge so full of lumps that it was nearly inedible. Ylva kept me only because Jorgen insisted.

I was about two years old when Jorgen, out fishing in the river, grabbed a strange, rough basket as it floated past. He found me inside, sound asleep. The river came down from the mountain glaciers and was ice-cold. If the basket had tipped in the swift current or leaked, I would have perished from the freezing water. But I was perfectly dry, and when I opened my eyes—the color of spring violets in this land of the blue-eyed—Jorgen was overcome with astonishment and could not leave me to the river. He carried me home to his new wife and two motherless children—his son, Kai, who was close to my age, or so they guessed, and his daughter, Karina, who was five years older. I had stayed with them ever since, but I certainly was not part of the family, and Ylva never let me forget that. I helped Kai with the shepherding, and Karina and Ylva with the household chores; and I slept on a pallet in the barn with the sheep. Ylva did not even let me eat at the table with the others.

Finally I stood and walked out across the fields, as

I liked to do at night when I could not sleep. It was a late spring evening, not long before Midsummer, the longest day of the year. For a week or two before and as long after, the sun did not set at all but hovered at the edge of the horizon, casting a weak glow over the night. My eyes were used to the dim light, and I could see in it almost as clearly as in daylight.

I tried to decide what I should do. I could not stay, I knew that. But where could I go? I had no family, no friends besides Kai and Karina. After hours of walking, I came up with a plan. As a baby I had come down the river from the north, and so I resolved that I would leave the next night and head back that way. Maybe there was someone upriver who knew me, an uncle or a cousin who might welcome me into his or her home. But why, I wondered, had no one ever come looking for me? This question had plagued me all my life. Who had placed me in the basket, and why? Had someone saved me from danger? Or had someone tried to kill me by putting me into the icy water?

I shook my head to clear it. Perhaps I would find the answers if I walked north. Perhaps I would even find a real family of my own.

At last my legs grew tired, and I headed back to the barn. I passed our nisse, the little elf that lived under the house and protected the farm. Every farm I knew of had a nisse, all of them slight creatures in red caps, only a bit more than waist high, with long gray beards and pointed elvish ears. Some were more mischievous than others. When our nisse was annoyed—which was frequently—he would turn things upside down, from mugs to milk pails to beds; but he did not do any real damage. He did not like being seen, and we never spoke. In fact, if I stared at him or appeared to notice him in any way, he would get furious. His face would grow as red as his cap, and I would run back to the house as fast as I could, before he could turn *me* upside down. Sometimes I snuck a morsel of food and left it for him. I never saw him take it, but it was always gone soon after I left it. I was a little surprised to see him, as all the nisses disappeared for a time around Midsummer. No one knew exactly why, but I liked to imagine them having their own Midsummer's Eve celebration, scowling and grumbling and playing tricks on one another around a big Midsummer bonfire.

I dozed for a while in the barn among the warm, woolly sheep, and when the sky lightened I rose and went into the farmhouse. Before long I heard stirrings overhead in the loft, and the family descended, first Kai and Karina, then Jorgen, and finally, yawning and stretching, Ylva.

I met no one's eyes as I served them their breakfast of tea and porridge. I had decided not to tell anybody that I was leaving, yet I knew that if I looked at Kai or Karina, they would realize at once that something was dreadfully amiss. Ylva and Jorgen ate silently, but Kai ran his spoon through his porridge and said, "The lumps are only as big as pebbles today, Lilia! Have you lost your touch?"

Karina laughed, but I scowled at him. He gave me a quizzical look, and I looked away, hoping he could not read my thoughts.

After breakfast Kai stood and called Ove to him. "Time to take the sheep to pasture," he told the dog. "Are you ready, Lilia?"

I took off my apron and followed them outside. As we did every day, we opened the barnyard gate, and Ove herded the sheep up the hillside. As soon as they were grazing in the green fields, I headed to a clearing by a brook. Usually Kai and I stayed near the sheep, wandering the fields and talking, but today I longed to be alone. Kai did not take the hint, though, and followed me.

"I can tell you are upset," he said, settling himself beside me in the soft grass. "What is it? Did Ylva say something terrible?"

"When does your stepmother not say something terrible?" I retorted.

Kai laughed. "I meant something more terrible than usual."

I longed to tell him. Usually I told him everything. But I did not.

I lay back in the grass, hearing the calls of the sheep in the distance and Ove's occasional sharp bark as a lamb strayed from the flock. Far above I could see a bird circling—a hawk or a falcon, perhaps. In the North Kingdoms, I had heard, the huge falcons were a threat. A large one could carry off a newborn lamb, and many shepherds dreaded seeing them out hunting. But they never bothered our flocks here in the South, and I loved to watch them soar on the air currents that flowed far above the farm.

"Well?" Kai asked again, pulling my braid to get my attention. "Did she say something to upset you?"

I shook my head and closed my eyes, pretending to sleep. I could not think how to tell him what I had heard and what I planned. Before long I heard him sigh and rise and head back to the flock, and without meaning to, I fell truly asleep.

I soar like a bird, weightless. Below me I can see a river rushing through stands of pine trees, and beyond that, snow-capped mountains rise from a green plain. I look up, and the sky is changed. It is green, and blue, and the purple of wild lavender. The colors pulse with the rhythm of a heartbeat. I have never seen anything so strange, but I am not afraid.

"Lilia, wake up!"

Kai was shaking me, and I roused myself. It was time to bring back the sheep, and I knew I had much to do to prepare for leaving the farm that night. Our walk back was silent, but Kai cast sidelong glances at me, and I had to work hard to ignore the unspoken questions in his blue eyes. I could hardly bear to think of how much I would miss him, and when our hands brushed as we walked, I grabbed his and squeezed it. He grinned at me then, reassured, and I smiled at him.

Back at the farmhouse, we were surprised to see Ylva bustling around the kitchen, looking uncustomarily pleased and contented as she stirred the supper pot. Good smells rose up from the stove. Usually Ylva insisted that plain food was all that a body required, but perhaps in celebration of her decision to get rid of me, she had decided to add some herbs and spices to tonight's mutton stew. *Well, good riddance to you, too!* I thought resentfully. I would be glad never to see her again.

The family sat at the rough-hewn oak table, and I perched on a stool by the fire with my meal. Ylva ate two large bowlfuls, and Kai and Jorgen did as well. Even I was tempted to ask for a second helping, but I remembered Ylva's lies about eating them out of house and home and kept quiet.

"A fine supper, wife," Jorgen said approvingly when he was finished, reaching for his pipe.

"Why, thank you, husband," Ylva said in a flirtatious tone that made me wince. "Now in return, I need you to do something for me."

"At your service, madam," Jorgen said grandly. I exchanged a look with Karina, and rolled my eyes at her. She had to cover her mouth with a napkin to keep a laugh from escaping.

"I need the cradle from the shed," Ylva said. "I want to clean it and set it up right there, beside the fire."

"So soon?" Jorgen asked, pushing back from the table. "The baby is not due for months yet." With that, Ylva's good mood was gone.

"*Now*, husband!" she commanded.

Jorgen and Kai and I hurried out the door to the shed that housed tools and the items that would not fit in the small house. "I know it is in here somewhere," Jorgen muttered, holding a candle high to light the gloomy space and pushing aside hoes and rakes and scraps of wood.

I had not been inside the shed since I was a child, when Kai and I would use it in our games of hide-and-seek. Everything that was too broken to use but too valuable to throw away had been thrust inside. It was dark and musty, and the dust we disturbed made me cough. In the candlelight I could make out a broken chair, a child-sized bed frame, and a three-legged stool with only two legs remaining that leaned against the wall. Kai pushed the stool aside. "Father, what is that?" he asked, pointing.

I stared at the object, trying to figure out what it could be. It was shaped like a large bowl or a basket, but it seemed to be made of sticks, woven awkwardly together. The spaces between the sticks were daubed with clay, and strange materials—feathers, bits of wool—were stuck into the clay.

"My goodness," said Jorgen softly. "I think it is your basket, Lilia—the one I found you in."

"This is my basket?" I asked, astonished.

"I must have kept it. I hadn't remembered."

"The clay is as hard as stone," Kai observed, tapping it. "It still seems solid and watertight, even after all these years." He ran his hand over the basket's rough surface.

"Well," I said at last, looking at its outlandish construction, "I suppose this proves I am the daughter of the worst basket maker in the land!"

Kai and Jorgen both snorted with laughter, and Jorgen laid a hand on my arm. I imagined from his gentle touch that he was trying to apologize to me for what he knew must happen, and I put my hand over his as if to say *Yes, I know; I forgive you.*

With a little more searching, we found the cradle, a carved wooden piece that rested on a curved base so that it would rock side to side. We carried it out of the shed, and in the brighter light of the midsummer evening we could see that it was dusty and full of mouse droppings. I was set to work scrubbing it. Soon the cradle was clean and fresh smelling, and we moved it into the farmhouse, near the fireside as Ylva directed us.

Ylva climbed up to the loft, and I thought she was going early to bed, but she descended a few moments later, carrying something under her arm. As she shook it out, I could see that it was a child-sized blanket, woven in exquisite shades of green, blue, and violet. I gasped in shock, for it was exactly the colors of the sky in the dream I'd had earlier. I stepped forward to touch it. The wool was as soft as velvet, and when I felt it, I shivered, though I could not say why.

Ylva snatched it from my grasp. "Keep those dirty hands away!" she said.

"Where did this blanket come from?" I asked.

"I have been saving it for years for my own child," she told me.

Jorgen, who had been smoking his pipe by the fire, rose from his chair and came to look at the blanket.

"I have not seen this for over a decade!" he exclaimed.

"Lilia, this was your blanket. You were wrapped in it when I found you. You can see it is woven so tightly that not a drop of water could wet you through it. I'd quite forgotten we had it!"

"It is mine?" I inquired in awe.

"No, girl," Ylva retorted. "It is ours, and now it will keep our child warm." She stroked the blanket possessively, folded it carefully, and laid it in the cradle.

No, it is mine, I thought. My eyes were drawn to it, but I looked away quickly. I did not want to attract Ylva's attention.

I went out to the barn after the supper dishes were cleaned and waited until I was sure the family slept. Then I crept back into the house, carrying a small pack that already held my one spare dress and a kerchief. Without intending to, I tiptoed over to the cradle and pulled out the blanket, admiring it in the firelight. It was so beautiful; the colors flowed one into the next: green to blue, blue to violet, violet to darker purple. The wool was edged on all four sides with green satin ribbon, and it smelled sweet. I turned it over, looking for clues, for a mark—for anything that might trigger my memory or offer a hint of where it had been made— but there was nothing. The coverlets we used, though warm, were rough and scratchy; and as I rubbed the blanket on my cheek, I could not imagine how wool could be so soft. It felt delicious against my skin. *It is mine,* I thought again firmly, quickly stuffing it into my pack.

Now I needed food. I rummaged through the cupboards and took a small loaf of dark bread, some hard cheese, and some mutton that I wrapped carefully so it would not stain the blanket. The guilt I felt for robbing Jorgen was not hard to suppress. *Ylva has sold me,* I reminded myself over and over, thinking of the miller and his cruel eyes.

Before I left, I looked around the farmhouse one last time. It was a humble place, but it had been my home. Jorgen was as close as I had to a father, and Kai and Karina were my dear friends. I felt the press of tears, but my excitement was stronger than my regret.

I turned my back on the room, eased open the door, and left. The midsummer moon had risen and lighted my way brightly enough to show the stones and bushes that lined the path. I glimpsed the nisse scrambling over rocks as I climbed the hill to the pastures where Kai and I brought the sheep to graze. From there I knew I could see the farmhouse clearly below, but I did not want to look back. I was starting a new life. I looked forward, to the River Alfta and the North and the unknown—to *my* home.

2

A TRUE PRINCESS
DOES NOT PERFORM IN PUBLIC

I joined the road just outside Hagi but hesitated to enter the village, for I did not want people to wonder why I was out alone at such an hour. The suspicious townspeople already had a low opinion of me. Whispers of my mysterious origins often followed me through the streets, and no one felt any remorse about speaking ill of me, since I was only a servant to them. Still, to go around the village would add an hour or more to my journey, and I had already walked for miles. I decided to take my chances and go in through the stone gate.

Hagi was a homely place. Its few streets were dirt and its houses small and pressed close together. There was hardly anyone about; a few merchants walked sleepily toward the market, where they would peddle their wares when morning came. But I was unlucky enough to pass by one of the miller's sons, returning from a night of revelry. Konur stopped when he saw me.

"It is the foundling, Lilia!" he jeered, his fat face creased with a grin at his own great cleverness. "Soon you will have yet another home, won't you? Ylva says your cooking is very fine—we are all looking forward to it!"

I clenched my fists but kept walking, unwilling to dignify his comments with a reply; and Konur stumbled off, laughing. I thought that it would almost be worth going to the miller's just to see their faces when they tasted my cooking. I had to smile when I pictured Odur and his family trying to eat my lumpy porridge and rock-hard bread.

I was through the town quickly and out the far gate just after the early sunrise. Before long I left the path and found the small cave that Kai had discovered many years earlier. It was clean and dry, its floor hard-packed dirt and its rock ceiling low and snug. I settled myself, pulled out bread and cheese and slices of mutton. When night fell again, I would make my way to the river and begin to follow it northward. I would enter new territory then, for I had never in memory been farther from the farm than I was now.

It was the first moment I'd had to consider what I had done. I could hardly believe that I had found the courage to leave without a word or a backward glance. I was happy to leave Ylva behind, but I was beginning to realize how terribly I would miss Kai and Karina. Karina had always been as good to me as a real sister would be; and Kai and I had spent countless hours out in the fields talking, chasing after sheep, and playing games. We knew each other's dreams: his, to become something—anything—other than a shepherd; mine, to find my family and a home I could call my own. I let a few tears fall, but I stopped myself from giving in to sadness. Instead, I pulled the soft blanket out of my pack and wrapped it about my shoulders like a shawl. In a moment I fell asleep, leaning against the cave wall.

A group of men, dressed in fine silks and velvets, ride on horseback across a green field. The sun is high, and it glints on one man's golden crown. He carries an enormous falcon, a bird so large that it seems his arm could hardly bear its weight. All at once the riders halt, and the king—for a king he must be—raises his arm. The falcon takes flight, its heavy wings beating and beating until it is only a speck in the azure sky. The men shout, and the bird plunges toward earth. Just before it will surely crash to the ground it sweeps upward, a rabbit in its sharp talons. The men clap and call out their praise, and another horse gallops near. On this white steed is a woman, her long skirts flowing as she races toward the group. She comes nearer. . . .

I woke suddenly. I had dreamed of this dark-haired woman before but never was able to see her face. She was forever moving—on horseback, or dancing, or walking through gardens with a gait so graceful that she almost seemed to float.

Then I realized that something had awakened me: there was a strange noise outside the cave. It was a sort of snuffling; a creature was moving near the entrance. Thoughts of wolves sent a shiver through me. As stealthily as I could, I crept to the front of the small cave, grabbing a stick as I moved. My hand trembled as I peered into the dimness.

Suddenly a beast leaped forward, knocking me back into the cave. I screamed in terror, feeling wetness on my face. But a moment later I realized it was not a wolf, and the wetness was not blood. My attacker was Ove, and he was licking me wildly with excitement and joy. Behind him, Kai and Karina were shaking with laughter. I struggled to retain a shred of my dignity.

"Bad dog!" I scolded. "What are you doing here? You should be guarding your sheep!" Ove grabbed the stick I'd dropped and offered it to me. He cocked his head to the side in a way that was almost human, showing that he was listening hard. Kai laughed even harder.

"What *are* you doing here?" I asked Kai, crawling out

of the cave to stand upright. "How did you find me?"

Kai smiled, proud of his dog's talent. "Ove did it," he said. "He pulled us right through town and straight here. I knew he could herd, but I didn't know he could track!"

Ove's tail wagged happily, and he sat on his haunches and panted, as if pleased by the praise.

"But . . . ," I said helplessly. "I am going north, you see."

"And you didn't tell us," Karina said reproachfully. "We should be very angry at you."

"I'm sorry," I said, looking at Kai. "I felt dreadful saying nothing to either of you. But I had to go."

"We know that," Kai said gently. "When Papa discovered that you had left, he told us why. You could not go to the miller. He understood that."

"But you cannot go wherever you are going alone either," Karina added. "We are going with you."

I gasped. "That's impossible! What about your father—and your stepmother? They will never let you go!"

"Ylva wouldn't have let you go either, not when she was expecting payment for you," Kai noted wryly. "Yet you went nevertheless. And you took the blanket!" He pointed to it, still wrapped around my shoulders. "Ylva was so angry about it that she turned on us both. She forgot she wanted Karina to help her with the baby and threatened to betroth her to the miller's son—that pig Konur."

I looked at Karina, horrified. "Your father would never allow that," I exclaimed.

"I think he would not," Karina replied, her lips trembling slightly, "but who can say, when Ylva wants something? And even if it did not happen, I do not want to be nursemaid to Ylva's baby, though it will be our half-brother or -sister. I would have had all the work of it, while Ylva sat like a queen and kissed the babe good morning and good night."

Kai added, "And I—I do not want to tend the sheep without you." His voice was soft, and I looked at him with surprise.

"It would be boring," he went on, scuffing his foot in the dirt. "I would have no one to talk to but Ove, and he rarely answers."

"But your father," I protested weakly. "Can you leave him like that?"

"Karina and I talked about it when we found you had gone," Kai replied, sighing. "Father has his new family now. Without our three mouths to feed, he can hire a hand to help him with the farmwork—someone who would do better than you and I together, no doubt!"

I imagined Ylva's wrath when she discovered that all

three of us were gone. It was a shame to miss that spectacle, and I smiled at the thought.

"Will you have us as your traveling companions?" Kai asked uncertainly.

"Will I have you?" I cried. "It would be wonderful! I was so afraid to go by myself—you know I would dream as I walked and probably fall off a mountainside. Karina can show us the best places to make our camp, and you can protect us—it will be grand!"

He laughed, relieved. "And what will you do?"

I shrugged. "Tell you tales, perhaps?" He liked it when I told him my dreams as if they were stories. "Sing you songs? Cook our porridge?"

He shook his head. "Your porridge is dreadful," he teased me. "Really, Karina's is much better. I've never understood why Ylva had you make it each morning."

"She did it to torture me," I said. "She knew I was bad at it, and she knew I hated to do it, so of course it was my job. Oh, imagine no more Ylva!" I twirled around with happiness, and they laughed at my joy.

"I think for a time, at least, we should walk by night in case Ylva sends someone after us," I said finally.

Kai smiled. "You will have to lead us then, Lilia. We are not used to walking in the dark."

I was pleased that there was something I could do to help. "It is nearly Midsummer," I reminded him. "It will be light until very late. And the moon is waxing as well. It will light our way, and it will get fuller each night. Walking should not be difficult."

"Not for you, perhaps," Kai said wryly, "but I do not have your falcon's eyes, and you know that Karina is scared of the dark. You will have to be our guide."

"But we may see people, even at night. What then?" Karina asked, her practical mind ever working.

"We will walk near the edge of the road," I replied, "so we can hide if need be. But who would be out so late?"

"Robbers and brigands," Karina answered gloomily. "Bears. Wolves."

Kai snorted. "There are no bears this far south," he informed his sister. "And wolves are more afraid of us than we are of them in this season. Besides, I do not fear brigands!" He waved the knife he carried to cut bread and cheese—our only weapon. Karina and I exchanged a doubtful look and then burst out laughing. A shepherd's knife would do little to protect us against a band of thieves with swords.

"We have nothing to steal anyway," I pointed out.

"True enough," Kai acknowledged. "Now I think we should rest for a while, and then you can lead us onward."

They curled up on the rough cave floor and were

soon asleep, but I went outside with Ove. We found a small stream that fed the nearby river, and I washed my face while Ove drank. Then we went back to the cave and waited for the dimming of the light that was midsummer nightfall. I roused Kai and Karina, and we shared some of the food they had brought. At last I stuffed my blanket back into my pack, and we started out. As we walked, I told them about the dream I'd had before they came.

"Can people really hunt with falcons?" Karina asked.

"I am sure that kings do," I said. "I once heard a peddler in town tell about such a royal hunt."

"But falcons are so big!"

"Birds are very light, even the big ones," Kai pointed out. "I think it could be done. I recall that story—that must be where you got the idea, Lilia."

I nodded. I loved and remembered all the tales I heard from passing traders or minstrels of the doings of royalty. And of course they found their way into my dreams.

Before long we rejoined the wide dirt road, which ran along the River Alfta. My plan, which Kai and Karina approved, was to keep traveling that road until we passed from the South Kingdoms into the North Kingdoms. The few people we had seen in Hagi who came from the north had dark hair, like mine, so I felt that perhaps we shared a kinship. I stared at the slow-moving green river and ran over to dip my fingers in its icy waters. This, I thought with a flutter of excitement, might be the path that would lead me to my family.

We spent the next several days on the road. On our right was always the river, sometimes obscured by trees. The sound of its rushing waters was the musical accompaniment to our long hours of walking.

I found that our strange schedule suited me well. During the day we lay on the ground, sheltered from the road and any passers-by. Since I did not have to lie in a bed, I was actually able to sleep, especially if I wrapped myself in the multicolored blanket. I woke rested and alert. Sounds and sights became clearer to me, no longer viewed through a haze of exhaustion. The world took on a brighter hue, and I was far happier than I had been at the farm. Once Kai and Karina got over their initial soreness from walking and sleeping on the ground, they too seemed to enjoy the journey.

But our contentment did not last. Our food supply began to run low, and then clouds moved in and light rain started to fall. Walking became a misery as the road grew muddy and the rain came down harder. When we saw the lights of a small town in the distance, we hurried toward it to find shelter.

"What shall we do if someone wonders why we are traveling alone?" I gasped as we dashed through the puddles.

"I will say I am taking you both up north, to relatives, should anyone ask," Karina replied. "It is not really a lie."

The rain dripped off my nose as we slogged through the town gates. We were immediately drawn to the candlelight in the windows of a tavern. A sign above the door showed a large, badly painted bird and proclaimed the inn the Falcon's Roost. When Kai pushed open the door, we were met with the sound of cheerful voices and the mingled smells of food and ale. I breathed in deeply, feeling the warmth from the welcoming fire at the end of the long room.

All eyes turned to us as we entered. I was sure that questions would be asked at the sight of three young people and a dog traveling alone. But the men were well into their cups, as it was late, and the serving maid, a plump woman in a grease-streaked apron, greeted us with a smile.

"'Tis late to be out, and so wet!" she exclaimed. "You must be hungry. Let me dry your cloaks by the fire. Some stew, a cup of cider?"

I looked questioningly at Kai, for I had no money. He

pulled out a few coppers and asked, "Will this do?"

"That's enough for supper and a bed," said the woman. "Do you wish to spend the night?"

Karina nodded vigorously, water spraying from her braid. "Oh, please," she begged. "I long for a bed!"

"You girls can share, since you are the only females," the woman told us kindly. "And the lad can stay with the men. The dog must bide downstairs, though."

She took our rain-soaked cloaks and pointed us to a space at the long table. The men slid over to make room for us on the bench. In a moment we had bowls of fragrant stew and mugs of warmed cider. The meat was strange but good; I was so used to mutton that I could not name it.

"'Tis reindeer," the serving maid, Sigrid, said when we asked. "It makes a fine stew, doesn't it?"

We nodded with enthusiasm, eating as fast as we could, and Ove gulped his food down by the fire. When at last we pushed our bowls away, we were full for the first time in days and beginning to dry out.

The men—I marked them as traders from the North Kingdoms by their full packs and dark hair—began to sing. Their voices were rough, but their songs were like stories, and we listened, enthralled. After two songs, a trader turned to me, his dark beard flecked with foam from his ale.

"You must sing for your supper too, ladies!" he cried, and the others took up the call. "Sing! Sing!"

Karina was fearful and embarrassed, but I took her hand and stood. "We had better do as they ask," I whispered to her. We chose a song about a knight enchanted by elves. At first Karina's voice was weak and shaky, but mine was strong; and the attentive silence of our audience soon made her feel more confident. We harmonized well, and at the end the traders clapped and cheered and stomped their heavy boots, and we bowed our heads, pink with pleasure.

Then, from the far end of the table, a short, bearded man spoke up. "I know an elf song as well," he said. He was one of three, all richly dressed and obviously of high birth. Next to him sat a tall lord with a long, craggy face who shook his head at his friend's words.

The third companion, a lord in a dark blue cloak, protested sharply. "No, that one is too dark, Erlend; it will frighten the ladies." I noticed that his eyes were on Karina. But the traders called again, "Sing! Sing!" and so Sir Erlend began.

"Who rides there so late through the night dark and drear?
The father it is, with his infant so dear;
He holds the boy tightly clasped in his arm,
He holds him there safely, he keeps the boy warm.

" 'My dearest son, why do you try so to hide?'
'Look, father, the Elf-King is close by our side!
Do you not see him, with crown and with train?'
'My son, 'tis the mist rising over the plain.' "

Sir Erlend's voice was clear and pleasing, but shivers ran through me as he sang more stanzas telling of the father's desperate ride to save his son from the grasp of the Elf-King, and finally finished the song:

"The father now gallops, with terror half wild,
He grasps in his arms the poor shuddering child;
He reaches his courtyard with toil and with dread,—
The child in his arms he finds motionless, dead."

3

A True Princess
Moves with Measured Grace

At the end of the song there was utter silence. All I could hear was the crackling of the fire. Then Ove whimpered in a dream and the spell was broken. The men laughed and began to talk again. Sir Erlend turned to us.

"They say 'tis a true story," he told us, his eyes twinkling above his trim beard.

"It's a very terrible tale," I said. "I would hate to meet the Elf-King." We had heard little about him in Hagi, but I knew he was a creature of the North Kingdoms.

"Are you going north?" Sir Erlend asked. We nodded.

"Then beware of Bitra Forest, for it is said that is

where the Elf-King bides."

"Does he only take children?" Karina asked nervously. "For we are all beyond childhood, and should be safe."

"I know only what the song says," Sir Erlend replied.

The lord in blue interrupted him. I could see that his eyes, like mine, were violet, and I thought, *He must be from my homeland!* "There is danger on the road and in the forest," he warned, "both human and elvish."

"Do you believe the stories, sir?" Karina asked, looking at him. He met her eyes and smiled. I saw her blush, but she smiled back at him.

"I do, lady. I know that the Elf-King rules the forest, and I have heard the sound of the horn and the baying of the hounds in Odin's Hunt."

"Odin's Hunt? What is that?" I asked.

The blue lord answered courteously, "The story differs depending on who tells it. Odin is a spirit, or a fairy, or a supernatural being of some sort—no one knows for certain. But he is an immortal. His Hunt is a sign of danger, or of bad times, or at least of change. If you witness the Hunt passing, they say, you will die within a fortnight. Even if you just hear the passing, your life will surely change."

"And you, sir," I said hesitantly. "When you heard it,

did your life change?"

His face darkened, and I thought to apologize for my boldness, but again he replied.

"It did, milady. I was just a child when I heard the Hunt pass. I knew the stories, so I covered my eyes and hid behind a tree. I did not see Odin and his eight-legged horse and his black dogs. But I heard him, and after—ah, then everything was changed." His voice was so sad that I felt tears start in my eyes, and when I looked at Karina I could see that she too was moved.

"I am sorry, sir," I said softly. "I did not mean to pry."

"And the Elf-King," Karina said, trying to change the course of the conversation. "Is he a danger only to children?"

"Yes," said the lord. "He is a terrible threat to infants and children alike, but they say he does not take anyone past the age of seven. We call those he has taken changelings, though he does not leave any of his own kind in their place. None is ever seen again."

Sir Erlend added, "But his daughter, milady! It is said that the Elf-King's daughter is the most beautiful creature that has ever existed. For a man to look on her is to risk enchantment—and even death."

"But the elves will not go on the road, will they?" Karina asked fearfully.

"No," the blue lord replied. "They live deep, deep inside Bitra Forest. They will not travel on paths that humans have created. On the road you are safe—from elves, at any rate." The lord reached into a saddlebag that rested on the floor beside him. He pulled out a blade—a short, straight sword, much smaller than the jeweled sword at his side but much larger than Kai's stubby knife. Then he came over and held out the sword to Kai.

"Sir," he said to Kai, who seemed surprised at such an address. "Will you take this sword to protect your companions? Thieves travel the road, preying on the unwary; and many a tinker, trader, and traveler has lost his belongings, or even his life." I glanced again at Karina and saw my own unease reflected in her face.

Kai stood and bowed. "My lord," he said, grasping the sword's hilt, "I will take it, but only for our journey. I would return it to you after we have reached our destination."

"And what is your destination?" the lord asked.

"The North Kingdoms," Kai replied. He held the blade aloft and admired its shine.

The lord smiled. "We are from the North Kingdom of Dalir and will be returning there within the month. Stop in Gilsa Town, which is not far after the road emerges from the forest, and ask for Sir Erlend. You can return the sword to him."

"I am grateful, my lord," Kai said, bowing again, "and I am at your service."

"And I at yours," the lord replied, bowing too. Karina and I rose and curtsied, I deeply and Karina with an awkward wobble. Then the lord paid Sigrid in shiny coppers and left the inn with his companions, though it was still raining outside. We stared after them open-mouthed.

"Well," Kai said finally when the door had closed behind them. "That was strange."

"Indeed it was," I agreed. "And now you have a sword!"

"But no idea how to use it," Kai said ruefully, and we laughed, the traders laughing with us. "We should sleep," Kai said then. "We have a long journey yet."

"So you are headed to the kingdom of Dalir?" asked one of the older men.

I nodded. I did not know Dalir, but something about it sounded right to me.

"Ah, you shall have to try your hand at the contest!" he boomed, and the others laughed.

"What contest? I asked.

"The king and queen of Dalir have decided that their son, Prince Tycho, shall wed, so they have offered to interview prospective brides," the trader told us. "But they will not accept just any lady, oh no!" The others nodded their heads in agreement. "They require a true princess, and there are not many of those in the North Kingdoms. So the ladies who come to call must pass a test."

"What test?" Karina asked, intrigued.

The man shrugged. "Who knows? Archery, writing, singing, manners—whatever it is that princesses do that the rest of us do not. Thus far they have had no luck at all."

"No luck," the men murmured.

"But you, my beauty—you look royal enough for anyone!" The trader swept low in a bow before Karina, spilling his ale and almost losing his balance. The other men roared, and with that, Karina and I allowed Kai to hurry us away from the table and up the steep staircase.

Our room was low-ceilinged and rather damp. The furnishings—a bed, a rickety table, a wobbly stool—were rough-hewn. There was a looking glass on the wall, though, and I stood before it as I sometimes had before the wavy glass of the mirror at the farm, wondering at the girl who looked back at me. She seemed such a stranger, with her odd-colored eyes and dark hair.

The bed was lumpy as all beds seemed to be, and I knew I would not sleep; but I climbed in with Karina anyway. She sighed with pleasure, though I squirmed as the mattress bunched beneath me.

"That lord was handsome, was he not?" she said dreamily, a smile on her face. I looked at her, surprised.

"The one in the blue cloak? Handsome? Well . . . I suppose he was. If you like dark hair," I said.

"Your hair is dark, Lilia," she retorted. "There is nothing wrong with dark hair. And what a kind face he had!"

I smiled. It was unlike Karina to be so romantic, but then, when had she had the chance before? On the farm we saw no one, and in Hagi we knew all our neighbors too well. It was impossible to dream of fat Konur; or the cobbler's son, Lars, with his lank hair and mottled skin; or Stig, the son of the butcher, who always smelled of fresh blood and sometimes sported streaks of it on his shirt as well.

"But what do you think of this prince of Dalir?" I asked. "Should we go there and present you as a possible bride?"

Karina laughed. "Me? A princess? I do not have any royal skills to help me pass the test. They'd throw me out on my ear!"

"Well, you can cook a fine meal," I pointed out. "And sew a small stitch, which is more than most princesses can do, I'm sure."

She made a face at me, and I warmed to my teasing. "But I guess that doesn't matter since you love the blue lord!"

"Oh!" she sputtered, and reached out to tickle me in revenge. I leaped out of bed to avoid her pinching hands and began to pull on my boots.

"Don't leave, Lilia," she begged.

"I'm going to make sure Ove is settled," I said. "I'll be back later."

"Oh, all right." She sank back into the pillows with a sigh of contentment, and I went out. From the top of the staircase I could tell that all was silent below. I crept down and saw that the candles were blown out and the tables cleared and cleaned. The traders had retired for the night. By the fire, Ove lay coiled in a tight circle, and he raised his head and wagged his tail as I approached.

"It's nice to be indoors out of the rain, isn't it, boy?" I whispered, and his tail thumped, *Yes, yes it is.* I took my cloak, dry now, from the peg near the fireplace and covered myself with it. Then I curled up with my head pillowed on Ove's flank and tried to sleep.

In the morning Kai came down before the traders, who were sleeping off their ale. He looked tired.

"They all snored, every last one," he complained. "And there were only three beds for the ten of us.

I'm half deafened and bruised all over—my bedmates kicked."

"Poor Kai!" I said with mock sympathy, and he grinned.

"At least it was a real bed, and not a dog for a mattress," he allowed. "I do think, though, that we should go right away. From what the gentlemen said last night, it sounds like we have more to fear at night than in the daytime. And people do not seem to take it amiss that we are traveling alone."

I knew he was right. "I'll wake Karina," I said, and hurried up the stairs. I found Karina fresh and rested, and we packed up quickly and gathered for a bowl of porridge.

"I still have some money left," Kai said when we had eaten. "I'll buy some bread and cheese." Sigrid was happy to sell him her leftovers, and she slipped in a little of the meat that had flavored our stew the night before. Then we started out, waving farewell to Sigrid as she stood in the doorway.

We walked down the road, now dry, past ramshackle shops and houses that leaned or sagged on their supports. Shopkeepers were sweeping at the front of their stores and arranging their goods for the day's customers, and we smiled at them as we went by. The townspeople were not as friendly as Sigrid and the traders, though. Most ignored us; some frowned or scowled because we were strangers, and we hurried our steps, relieved when we passed through the northern gate.

"Lilia," Karina asked me as we strode along, "where did you learn to curtsy like that?"

"Like what? I have never curtsied before in my life," I told her.

"At the inn last night, when we curtsied to the lords. You dipped so low," she said, trying it and wobbling so much that she nearly fell.

"Like this?" I inquired, curtsying. "Why, 'tis my natural grace, of course." Kai snorted with laughter and gave me a little push, and I fell over into the road and leaped up again to chase him, Ove barking behind us.

We walked for a day, passing at last from the South to the North Kingdoms. A carved wooden map marked the border, and we stood before it. A large section labeled "Bitra Forest" was just above the painted dot that showed where we stood.

"There is nothing there," Karina said in a low voice, looking at the vast expanse of woodland on the map. "No town, not even a village. Just woods."

I traced the road on the map as it ran between the river on one side and the forest on the other. "But here is Gilsa, just north of the forest, right where the lord said it was," I pointed out. "It is not so very far." I said this to calm Karina, for I could see that it was quite far indeed. Still, it was good to have a destination in mind.

The next morning a kindly trader gave us a ride on his wagon. We offered to share our food with him, but he waved our meager supplies aside, pulling out bread and meat enough for a dozen. "Sit and eat!" he invited us. We perched on rocks at the edge of the road and ate happily, tossing scraps to Ove, while the trader told us stories of his travels. His tales of encounters with bears in the North Kingdoms made Karina shudder, but it was another tale he told that unnerved me.

"Have you ever heard of the Elf-King?" I asked him, and he nodded, his mouth full.

"Indeed I have," he said after swallowing, "but luckily I have never come across an elf, even on my many trips through the forest. All I know of elves is songs and stories." He offered to sing the song we had heard at the inn, but we quickly declined. Then he told us, "There's many a tale of the Elf-King. Had you heard he slew a falcon?"

Our eyes big, we shook our heads. "Yes," the trader continued, "he shot it with an arrow. He did it just for sport, I heard tell. Just to show he could. Ever since then, the falcons have hated the elves—and who could blame them?" That chilled me, the idea of killing one of those majestic birds for no reason at all.

The trader turned west when a smaller road intersected the big one, telling us, "This is the last turnoff before Bitra Forest. Are you certain you want to keep going northward?" We nodded nervously and jumped off the wagon, and Ove leaped after us.

Waving farewell, the trader called, "Be sure to stay on the road!"

It stretched out ahead of us, and the river sparkled to our right. Far in the distance evergreen trees marked the edge of Bitra Forest. I remembered Sir Erlend's song and took a deep breath, trying to push it to the back of my mind. There were no other travelers on the road now, and we passed none as we tramped onward. It was nice to walk in the sunshine; but when we finally reached the trees, they nearly met overhead, blocking the sun's rays almost completely. Immediately the air seemed cooler.

"We must stay on the road," I reminded Kai, and he nodded. The evergreens rose up high above us. I had never seen such tall trees before. Our footsteps sounded loud on the dirt road. Fewer birds seemed to call; fewer squirrels chattered. Our conversation dwindled and then stopped entirely, and I caught myself looking right and left, before us and behind us—though I did not know why. I had the strange feeling that the forest had taken us captive.

"I don't like this," Karina said anxiously.

"Well, it's where the road goes, so we must follow," Kai replied. "And remember the map—on the other side is Gilsa."

The meager light from the sun filtered through the thick trees and did not warm us. As the hours passed, it lowered in the sky, but it did not set. I realized that Midsummer's Eve was near—was it in three days? A week? I had lost track of time in the days since we had left the farm. We prepared to stop and were looking for a spot where we could rest when suddenly something in the forest made a noise. It was a howl, or a shriek—a terrible sound. Ove, who ordinarily was a most obedient dog, leaped off the road and into the underbrush.

"Ove!" Kai shouted, and without thinking, he too dashed off the road. Karina and I stopped, unsure of what to do. I listened hard, but the forest had swallowed them as if they had never existed.

"Kai!" I cried, hoping my voice would guide him back. "Ove! Here, boy! Ove, Kai, where are you?" There was no answering call.

"Should we follow them?" Karina asked uncertainly. "Or should we wait?"

"Wait," I said decisively. I was not going into that wilderness if I had a choice. We perched on our packs at the road's edge, but our uneasiness made us stand again and pace back and forth, trying to see Kai in the dimness beneath the thick trees.

Suddenly, in the distance, we heard the sound of hoofbeats and the jangle of swords. I grasped Karina's hand and pulled her off the road. My heart thumped wildly as we crouched behind a bush, watching to see who would appear. I bit my lip hard when I saw that the four riders who trotted toward us on horseback did not wear the fine clothing of gentlemen but the low-brimmed hats and dark cloaks of brigands. Trained to see enemies or victims at a distance, the men noticed us easily. From his tall mount their leader called, "Come out of hiding! It will be the worse for you if we have to bring you out by force!"

We rose, hands still clasped tightly. I tried not to show my fear. Karina too stood as tall as she could, and she pressed her lips together to keep them from quivering. The men hooted when they saw us.

"Ladies!" the leader said in a mocking voice. We were close enough now that I could see a ragged scar that crossed his cheek from the corner of his eye to his mouth. He dismounted, and behind him his men did the same. "Ladies traveling alone—how very unusual.

Are you brave, my dears, or are you simply foolish?"
His tone was light, but his eyes, beneath the brim of his
felt hat, were dark and threatening.

"We must run," I whispered, squeezing Karina's
hand in mine. She nodded very slightly.

The brigands drew near behind their leader, and I
could see the pockmarks on the cheeks of one and the
dust that streaked the cloak of another. As we readied
ourselves to turn and flee into the forest, though, we
heard a cry from behind us and then a wild barking.
Kai, his borrowed sword drawn, ran onto the road, Ove
beside him. The leader drew his own sword quickly, but
he was distracted by Ove nipping at his legs; and Kai
brought his blade down on the brigand's forearm. The
man howled in pain and dropped his weapon, grabbing at his wounded arm as the blood dripped down.
He kicked at Ove, who danced around him, growling
fiercely.

"Get them!" the brigand cried, finding his voice
again; and his men leaped forward, their own swords
drawn.

"Kai!" I screamed as the brigands bore down on
him.

"Run!" Kai called to us, and to Ove, "Herd, boy"—
the command he used when sheep were straying.
Immediately Ove dashed to us, pushing us into the

forest as he would have pushed wayward lambs.

Knowing his single sword and unpracticed arm were no match for the thieves, Kai turned and fled as well. The three of us and Ove crashed through the underbrush as fast as we could run, tripping over fallen logs and hidden rocks. We ran for what seemed like hours, though I am sure it was much less than that. At last we had to stop, and we bent over, gasping. We stood still until we could breathe more easily and tried to hear whether anyone had followed us.

The silence was eerie. No bird called; no breeze disturbed the heavy air of the forest. It was quieter than any quiet I had ever experienced. I looked around in the dim light. Everywhere the trees closed in, and there was no path to be seen. I could not see the sky, so I could not judge our position from the sun. Was the road to our right? Or had we run south, placing it on our left? Perhaps we had gone straight into the forest and needed only to go straight back—but which way was back? I turned in a circle, looking for clues, but there was nothing to hint at where we were or where we should go.

"No," I whispered, my low voice sounding loud in that still place. "Oh no. We are lost in Bitra Forest."

4

A True Princess
Does Not Climb Trees

We stood beneath the looming trees, filled with dread. Ove pressed against us, and Karina crouched down to put her arms around him. He whimpered; and when Kai shushed him, Karina stood and turned on her brother.

"Why did you run off?" she demanded, her voice echoing in the forest. "You left us to the mercy of those robbers! This is all your fault!"

"I'm sorry," Kai said wretchedly. "I was afraid we would lose Ove. I didn't think—"

"No, you didn't!" Karina snapped. I could see that she was using her anger to mask her fear, and I interrupted her sharp words.

"Kai saved us, Karina. He fought against all of them! Without him . . ." My voice trailed off. I didn't want to think of what might have happened.

Kai held up his sword. The blade was streaked with blood. "I cut a man," he said, low.

"And it's a good thing you did," I replied briskly. "Wipe off the blade, and let's start walking. We can't stay here."

Obediently, Kai looked for a patch of grass or a clump of leaves to clean the sword, but the ground beneath us was bare save for a layer of brown needles from the pine trees. No underbrush could grow in this sunless place.

"I have a kerchief here somewhere," I said, rummaging in my pack. I pulled it out, and Kai wiped the blade until it gleamed again. Then I buried the soiled kerchief beneath the pine needles and picked up the pack.

"Come on," I commanded. Kai and Karina seemed to be in a trance. "Come on! We must move!"

"Where?" Karina asked helplessly, gazing around. "How can we know which way to go?"

"We can't," I admitted. Then when I saw the panic in Karina's eyes, I said with a confidence I did not feel, "We will just have to walk, and hope that we are walking in the right direction."

We started out, moving slowly around the enormous tree trunks that stretched upward as far as we could see. As we walked, Kai seemed to return to himself; and finally he said, "I have heard that moss grows on the north side of trees."

We looked carefully at the trees we passed. "There," I said, pointing to a patch of green growing on one side of a great trunk. We found more moss on many of the other trees and used it as a guide, hoping it was sending us northward. I thought for a moment of Hansel and Gretel and their journey through the forest. If only we'd left a trail of breadcrumbs from the road! But then I remembered that birds had eaten Hansel and Gretel's breadcrumbs, and they had been lost anyway.

After what must have been many hours walking through an unchanging forest, we grew too weary to go on and stopped to eat and sleep. We had barely spoken again all that long day. We ate in silence too, sharing the little bit of bread and cheese that we dared to eat— for who knew how long we would be in this wood? Still hungry, we lay back with our packs as pillows, I with my blanket wrapped around me. The pine needles made a soft surface beneath us, and in moments Karina was asleep. Kai, though, lay staring blankly upward. I knew that he did not see the heavy branches above him but was repeating in his mind the slice of sword through flesh, the scream of the brigand and the sight of his blood.

"What you did was so brave," I said softly, and he turned his head to look at me. His eyes were clouded with misery.

"I've never hurt a person before," he said. "I have never wanted to."

"You have never had to," I reminded him. "You saved us—you know you did. We couldn't have fended off those men otherwise."

He nodded and sighed deeply. "I didn't know I was capable of that."

"Well, I for one am glad that you are," I told him. "And perhaps that thief will think twice before he attacks his next victim!"

"Perhaps," Kai allowed, the trace of a smile on his lips. He closed his eyes then, signaling that he did not want to talk about it more. I closed mine as well, and thought that I too had changed. I did not believe that I could use a sword on a man, but I no longer felt that I was the dreamy girl who fumbled with the dishes and forgot her chores. I could curtsy like a lady and sing in front of a crowd. I had forced Kai and Karina to walk through the forest. I felt stronger and more awake there, in that dark, uncanny place, than I ever had on the farm; and I hoped that my strength would help us find our way through Bitra Forest.

Before long I drifted into sleep.

A dirt field, and at each end of the field there is a man on horseback, both man and horse heavily armored. At the sound of a horn, the riders race toward each other. They carry heavy lances, and it is obvious that each means to use the lance to unseat the other. They meet in the middle of the field with a great crash and the neighing of frightened horses. One knight goes flying, landing with a thump and the jangle of armor on the hard ground. A moment later he struggles to his feet, and the onlookers clap and cheer. The mounted knight rides to a raised dais, doffs his helmet, and bows his head to the king and queen; the queen stands and lays on his brow a circlet of entwined leaves and flowers. Again the knight bows; again the lords and ladies clap and laugh and sip cool drinks from colored goblets as the sun shines down. . . .

When I opened my eyes, I was met by the same gloomy dimness as before. The silence was complete, but it was not a peaceful stillness. Indeed, it made me feel quite uneasy. I imagined elf-spies behind every tree, though we had heard or seen no sign of any living, moving thing. Sighing, I stretched and rose, patted Ove, and woke Kai and Karina. We had not yet passed a stream where we could drink or wash, and I was beginning to worry about finding water.

I told them of my dream as we walked through the

endless silent forest, elaborating on the parts I did not truly remember: the ladies' dresses, the number of trumpeters, the flowers in the winners' garlands. Kai winced as I described the jousting, but Karina said, "I wish that I could see such a tournament!" and asked for still more detail.

At last we heard a very welcome sound: the rush of a stream over rocks. Ove sprinted ahead; and before we could think to stop him, he was lapping happily at the clear brook water.

"Ove—," I started, but it was too late. I held Karina back from joining him; and when she looked questioningly at me, I said, "What if it is enchanted?" We had all heard tales of elves and their food that, once eaten, bound the eater to them. What if the water flowing through this elvish place had the same power? Karina's hand flew to cover her mouth in alarm, and we stared at Ove, hoping he would not suddenly sprout wings or turn into a mole or begin to recite rhymed couplets. He felt our intent gazes and turned to look at us. Tilting his head to the side in that way he had, he wagged his tail and barked sharply in a tone that clearly said, *Come on in! The water's fine!*

And we did. The water was fine indeed—delicious and cold. We splashed our faces and scrubbed our dirty hands, drank until our stomachs hurt, and sat beside the brook on the soft pine needles, refreshed.

"Have I grown pointed ears?" Kai asked me, and I laughed.

"Not yet," I said, "but I see that Karina's nose has turned into a duck's beak." Karina hooted and grabbed for me, and I sprang up and dodged around her, Ove following me and barking with glee. Chase was his favorite game, whether it was sheep or humans he pursued. We ran in circles, accusing one another of magical transformations: "You've grown a squirrel's tail!" Kai told his sister; and she shouted, "And you have the skin of a trout—and its smell!" At last we were spent and collapsed, laughing, on the ground. Filled with joy, Ove rolled over and over in the pine needles, and we laughed until we wept to see him shake and the needles fly in all directions.

"Oh," Kai gasped, wiping his eyes as we finally quieted. "It feels good to laugh! This place is so grim."

"If there are evil spirits or creatures, we have surely let them know that we are here," I pointed out, thinking of the elvish spies I had imagined earlier. "But no doubt they knew that anyway."

We walked on, but within minutes I noticed that Ove's ears were raised—a sign that he smelled or heard something out of the ordinary. As I watched him, I saw a ridge of fur down the middle of his back rise up as well. Kai too looked closely at his dog, and then we followed Ove's gaze. To our horror we saw a lone white wolf not far from where we stood.

"A wolf!" Kai cried. "To the trees!"

We dashed forward, looking for a trunk with branches low enough to grab, as more wolves leaped out of the shadows behind the first one. I could see, from the corner of my eye, that these were not the gray wolves of the sheep fields but larger, snow-white animals. Their teeth glistened as white as their coats as they ran, and Ove turned to fend them off, showing his own teeth as he tried to protect us.

Karina was first to reach an enormous fir tree with low-hanging branches. She jumped, grabbed a branch, and swung herself up. I followed, mutely cursing the skirts that tangled around my legs. Balanced on the lowest branch, we looked down in helpless terror.

Below us six white wolves ringed Kai and Ove in a silence more fearsome than their howls would have been. Their tongues hung out as they panted, and their sharp claws left gouges in the dirt as they moved closer. For a moment all movement stopped. Then, faster than I would have believed possible, Kai seized Ove and hurled him, as if he were no heavier than a stick, up to Karina. The force of the throw nearly knocked Karina off the branch, and I grabbed for her as she caught Ove, holding him tight as his paws scrabbled wildly in the air. Kai leaped for the branch where we perched just as the wolves sprang, their razor-sharp teeth gnashing just inches below his dangling legs. Pulling himself up, Kai took Ove from his sister and we climbed higher, away from the slavering jaws that snapped beneath us.

The tree branches were like a stepladder reaching upward, and I climbed frantically. Long after Kai and Karina had settled themselves on a wide branch far above the forest floor, I kept going, pulled by an urge I did not understand. I felt that I must see a glimpse of sky, feel the fresh wind on my face. At last the branches grew too small to bear my weight, and I had to stop. I peered upward, trying to see blue among the brown branches and green needles. Instead, just above me between two branches I spied an enormous nest. It was built of branches as a smaller one might be built of twigs, and it was held together with mud. I clambered a little higher, testing each branch to make sure it would hold me. When I could look inside the nest, I saw that scattered in the mud were feathers, fur, and scraps of wool. I gasped and wobbled wildly, my shock almost making me lose my grip on the tree trunk. The nest was the same size and shape as the basket that had carried me safely down the river.

Not a basket, made by the world's worst basket maker, but a nest! As I ran my hand along its rough edges, I saw Kai climbing up behind me. Speechless, I pointed at the nest. His eyes widened.

"It is just the same as the one at home!" he exclaimed.

There was a rustle above us, and we looked upward, grabbing at the tree trunk for balance. On a branch far too thin to hold us sat an enormous falcon. Its dark eyes were on me, and I was suddenly very glad that the nest was empty of chicks. I knew what a falcon would do to protect its babies.

"This is your nest?" I asked the bird. She did not startle or appear to notice my voice in any way, but her gaze was intent. It was not an unfriendly look, and I had a sudden thought. I bowed my head to her.

"If you—or one of your kind—helped me when I was a baby, I thank you," I said formally, feeling a little foolish for talking to a bird. But the falcon seemed to acknowledge my words, uttering a loud, high-pitched cry. Then she spread her enormous wings, somehow avoiding the thicket of branches around her, and soared upward. In a moment we heard her cry again, and from the sound I knew that she flew above the trees in the open sky.

Kai and I climbed down to rejoin Karina, who was

waiting safely with Ove in the crook of the tree. We rested there, speculating about the nest and trying not to think about the wolves that might still be lurking below. Karina told us they had slipped back into the forest; but Ove still twitched nervously, so we did not dare to descend.

"Perhaps a falcon plucked you from your mother's arms," Kai suggested, but Karina disagreed.

"No mother would let go of her babe, no matter how fierce the bird," she insisted.

"Maybe it rescued me from some terrible danger," I said.

"I suppose it is possible . . . but then, why place you in a nest?" Karina asked skeptically. "Why float you down the river?"

I shrugged, frustrated. It seemed that every clue I gathered about my past—the blanket, the nest—raised a dozen new questions. I despaired of ever finding all the answers I wanted.

"We should start off again," I said sharply. Ove had finally fallen asleep in Karina's lap, his ears twitching with his dreams, so I knew that the immediate danger had passed. We climbed down warily and walked more carefully than before, stopping often to look and listen; but there was no sign of the wolves.

Before long, though, we noticed something peculiar.

With every step, the air grew heavier and thicker. The trees seemed to waver, shimmering as far-off objects do when the sun is very hot, though it was cool in the forest.

Ove whined fretfully. "Is it going to storm?" Karina asked.

"I don't know what it is," Kai said. I felt that we were moving toward a thing unknown. Perhaps, I thought hopefully, we were nearing the end of the forest and would emerge to see the road and Gilsa Town.

But the feeling of strangeness grew. It became harder to breathe, and we began to feel dizzy and disoriented. Again I imagined eyes watching us, and I wondered if we might be walking into some sort of dark magic.

"I shall have to sit down soon," Karina said to me, gasping. I feared to stop, so I took one of her hands and Kai the other. We stumbled on.

At last, not far ahead of us, we could see a gap in the trees. We halted, breathing heavily. Kai pulled us behind a thick trunk, and I took firm hold of Ove. As our breath returned, a sudden shaft of light illuminated the clearing, and we stared in astonishment at what we saw. In the center of the glade was a great rectangular table, made of silver or a silvery wood, with ornate carved legs. The table was set with golden plates and golden forks and knives, and a ruby-colored goblet graced each place. Enormous silver candelabra were placed at intervals down the table. The chairs too were carved silver, and at the far end of the table there was a throne of gold.

"Oh my," Karina said faintly.

We watched in silence as figures with pointed ears and green-tinged skin emerged from the surrounding forest.

"Elves," I whispered.

Dressed in fur and velvet, silk and satin, they noiselessly took their places at the table, standing behind their chairs. The candles all lighted in unison, and then the Elf-King came into the clearing.

5

A True Princess Is Not Demanding

e knew him at once, from the song and the story, and by his magnificent golden crown and fur-trimmed robe. He was tall and slender, and his face was very beautiful; but even from a distance I could see that the slash of his mouth was cruel. I peered around the tree to see more clearly, though I knew without being told that it was dangerous to spy upon the Elf-King. If we were discovered, he would surely not be forgiving.

At the Elf-King's right side was his daughter. It almost hurt to look at her perfection: her silvery hair that fell to her knees in waves, her exquisite face, her lithe figure. She moved with the sway of a willow, and she wore a dress of willow green, made of a material silkier and more flowing than any I knew. Like her father she was crowned with gold, and she too had a mouth that hinted at heartlessness.

I turned to Kai, suddenly afraid, recalling something Sir Erlend had told us—that he who looks upon the Elf-King's daughter risks enchantment, or even death. What I saw in Kai's face made my heart sink. He was gazing at her with such delight and pleasure, I felt that I might weep. I took his hand and squeezed it, but he showed no sign that he felt my touch. He had seen the Elf-King's daughter, and as we had been warned, he was lost to us.

Then Kai moved out from behind the tree that sheltered us and headed straight to the banquet table. Alarmed, I grabbed for him, but he shrugged me off and continued forward. Karina and I followed, not knowing what else to do, and Ove trotted behind.

The elves betrayed no surprise, and in a flash each elvish courtier held a bow with an arrow at the ready, pointed at us. Had they known we were there all along? Karina and I stopped, but Kai walked on, seemingly oblivious of the danger. He reached the Elf-King's daughter and went down on one knee, bowing his head and offering her the sword that the blue lord had given him. All was as silent and still as a painting.

Then the Elf-King's daughter laughed, a sound as delicate as wind chimes but somehow mocking. I felt a laugh rising in my own throat and forced it down, staring at the elvish princess. How could she make me want to laugh?

"Look, Father," the Elf-King's daughter said. "It is a human, come to me for Midsummer's Eve!" She clapped her hands in delight, and the other elf ladies at the table clapped too as one of the courtiers stepped forward and took Kai's sword from his unresisting hands.

Midsummer's Eve, I thought. Of course it was! I had lost track of the time, but I had known the longest day of the year was near. It explained the feeling of magic thick in the forest, the elves' banquet and celebration. Every town and village in the land celebrated this wildest of nights, most with a bonfire and dancing. Midsummer was a magical time, an occasion for fun and feasting, for healing spells and love charms. Many illnesses were cured, and many maidens found their husbands, on Midsummer's Eve.

The Elf-King looked at Kai. Then his glance slipped over Karina and landed, most fearfully, on me. I could not bear his gaze and stared at the ground. But a moment later the pointed, embroidered shoes of the

Elf-King appeared in my field of vision, and I knew he was standing directly in front of me. I dipped low in a curtsy, and he raised me with a hand under my chin.

"Who are you, girl?" he asked me, fixing his green eyes on me.

"Lilia, Your Majesty," I said, trembling.

"Hmmm," he murmured. "I think not. I think I know you. I think you once were mine."

"Yours?" I whispered.

"A day ago, a year ago, a decade ago, I took a baby girl with eyes like spring violets. Were you that child?" He searched my face, looking for clues. While he looked on me, I could not lie.

"I do not know," I said.

"I took that babe—but she was taken from me. The only one I have ever lost! Was that you?"

"I do not know," I said again.

Finally he glanced away from me, and I breathed in deeply. "It is too late now," he said dismissively. "The young ones can be controlled, but you are far too old to be biddable. Yet you have interrupted us and seen what you should not have seen. You must stay and be our captives."

With that careless command, the elf archers were on us, and in an instant Karina and I had our arms bound and were tied to a tree. We pulled hard against the ropes that held us, but we could not loosen them. Ove lay beside us limply, as if enchanted, his head on his paws.

Kai was given a place at the table, for the Elf-King's daughter clearly thought he was a fine plaything. She sat beside him and fed him tidbits from each of the countless courses that the elves' servants began to bring to them.

Dish after dish of the most marvelous and exotic fare came to the table. There was peacock, roasted whole and displayed with its feathers fanned. There was an enormous savory pie that, when the Elf-King's daughter cut into it, released a flock of warbling yellow birds. I thought again of Hansel and Gretel, and the memory of what happened to them when they ate the enchanted gingerbread house kept me from yearning too much for the feast I saw.

As the courses moved past us, I tried to undo the cords that held us to the tree. "Karina," I whispered, "can you reach the knot on my rope?" She struggled, but the ropes were too expertly tied, and again we sagged against the trunk.

Then I began to observe the servers. Many of them were nisses, their faces sour and scowling beneath their red caps. I recalled then how the nisses in our area disappeared each year at Midsummer, and I realized that

they all must be summoned—unwillingly, it seemed—
to serve at this yearly banquet. Karina too must have
noticed, for she whispered, "Look!" I followed her gaze
and saw our own nisse, carrying a crystal decanter of
ruby wine, his frown as pronounced as if it were bit-
ter vinegar. I caught his eye, and to my surprise he
looked directly at me and gave a tiny nod and a wink.
My heart lightened, just a little. He was our own nisse,
after all, pledged to protect us. Perhaps he could help.
But did that pledge hold so far from the farm? And if
it did, was there anything a nisse could do against the
immense power of the Elf-King?

I was distracted from my thoughts then as I saw a
different kind of server come into view, staggering
beneath his platter. The silver oval held an enormous
fish roasted whole, with a smaller roasted fish emerg-
ing from its mouth, and a still smaller fish spilling
from that one's mouth, and so on and on until the last
fish, a roasted minnow so small that it could barely be
seen. The dish was extraordinary, and the servant who
carried it was a child, a human boy, barely bigger than
the largest fish on his serving dish. I nudged Karina,
and she nodded. She had seen him too. *It is a changeling!*
I thought. Was the Elf-King telling the truth? Had I
once been a changeling too?

More children came into the clearing now. Some

carried delicacies: a spun-sugar cake in the shape of a palace, with sugar turrets flying ribbon-candy flags, and mounds of candied fruit in colors so vivid that it pained the eyes to look on them. Some stood on tip-toe to remove dirty cutlery and replace it with clean forks and knives and spoons. Some, the very youngest, washed the elves' hands with soft cloths.

"Look at their clothing," I told Karina urgently. "Many are wearing garments that have not been seen for decades, or even longer." There were toddlers in long, rough-made woolen shirts and young children wearing wooden shoes. Girls wore dresses with bodices or skirt lengths that had gone out of fashion before Ylva was born, and boys were in knee breeches from days long past.

"I can't make sense of it," Karina replied, watching the children and their strange garb.

The elves ate and drank and made merry. Elvish minstrels played on harps and lutes, and tumblers pranced across the soft grass that grew in the clearing. Even as hungry, tired, and frightened as we were, we found it a marvelous show; and I realized I had stopped straining to get away.

At last the elves were satisfied. The nisses and children removed the empty platters and dishes, leaving only the goblets. The Elf-King rose from his golden throne, holding his glass high.

"A toast," he cried in a voice like music. "On this Midsummer's Eve, we drink to the sun!"

The elves cried, "To the sun!" raised their goblets, and drank. Then the nisses carried away the long, heavy table and chairs and brought wood for a bonfire. With a word from the Elf-King, the fire lit itself, and its flame roared up through the gap in the trees that marked the clearing. Karina and I could feel the blaze's heat, and we shrank back against the tree.

The Elf-King and his courtiers disappeared with Kai into the woods; and the ladies, led by the Elf-King's daughter, began to dance about the bonfire. Like their leader, all were tall and silver haired and dressed in shades of green, but none matched the beauty of the Elf-King's daughter. Around and around they went, casting herbs into the flames with each circle they made. Together they chanted the names of the herbs they threw: "Orris and herb of grace; dog rose and verbena. Plumeria and elder flowers; savory and avena." Each herb caused the flames to roar upward and turned them a different color: orange, cobalt, deep purple, scarlet.

Karina and I exchanged glances. This dance was familiar to us, something we had seen many times. Karina had even been a part of it once or twice. I wondered if the purpose of the dance was the same here as it was in our village. For us, it was intended to show us our future husbands. The first male a girl saw after the dance was supposed to be her truelove. Of course, the boys and young men of the village knew to hide away from those girls they did not like, or to try to place themselves in the path of the ones they fancied, when the dance was ended. It was all a game, a part of the wild, joyous celebration of Midsummer, and no one took it seriously.

Here and now, though, the dance seemed very serious indeed. The elf women did not laugh or even smile as they circled the bonfire, and the face of the Elf-King's daughter was set with purpose.

At the height of the dance, I felt a tug on my arms and was shocked to see our nisse. His face was grimly determined as he struggled with our bindings. Our wrists were rubbed raw where we had pulled vainly against the ropes, but the nisse had some small elvish magic to work with, it seemed. In a rasping voice he muttered strange words as he toiled, the first I had ever heard him speak. In a few minutes we were free, and we crept backward with the nisse, our eyes still fixed on the wild dance.

"Run," the nisse commanded. "Run, and do not look back. Never tell what you have seen."

Oh, how I longed to obey! But I remembered the changelings, the poor babies and children who must be missing their families. How could I leave them there? And I ached to think of Kai, his merry blue eyes and blond curls and the smile he saved only for me. I thought of the way he had looked when he'd said he did not want to herd sheep without me, and I knew all at once that I did not want to do anything—anything at all—without him. No, we would not abandon him to the Elf-King's daughter.

"We must get Kai," I said, and Karina nodded in agreement.

"He is lost to you," the nisse said matter-of-factly. "There is nothing you can do for him. You can only save yourselves, you foolish girls."

"He is not lost," I said with a decisiveness I did not feel. "We'll not go without him."

The nisse rolled his eyes. "Humans!" he said, with both scorn and pity in his tone. "I cannot help you, then. I wish you luck, for you will need it!" With that he disappeared into the woods, and at that moment the music and wild movement of the dance ended.

The Elf-King's daughter looked to the trees opposite us. Kai appeared, his face expressionless, and walked over to her as if pulled by an invisible chain. When he reached her, she placed a delicate hand atop Kai's blond curls and spoke one word:

"Mine."

Karina and I both cried out "No!" in a single breath. Ove barked furiously. But at a glance from the Elf-King's daughter, he subsided and lay on the ground, whimpering. The ladies looked at us in great surprise.

"No?" the Elf-King's daughter repeated gently. She laughed, a sound so lovely and contagious that again I had the urge to laugh as well and suppressed it only with the greatest effort.

"He—he is my brother," Karina stammered.

"Then you shall be my dearest sister," the Elf-King's daughter said fondly to Karina. She laughed again, and despite myself I smiled. A look of tremendous confusion passed over Karina's face. I thought that in her place I might give in, for the notion of being sister to the Elf-King's daughter seemed at that moment something greatly to be desired. But I struggled against the idea; I would not give in to the elvish magic. Resolutely, I stepped forward.

"He is human, a mortal," I said. "He is not one of you. You cannot have him."

"I cannot?" the Elf-King's daughter repeated. "I cannot? I *cannot*?" Her face twisted and changed in her fury, and all at once I could glimpse on her lovely features shadows of the terrible things she had seen and done in her endless lifetime. She seemed to grow larger and larger as her rage increased, and she towered above us as we shrank away from her. She raised her arm, and I was sure that whatever magic she summoned would be the end of us.

"Daughter, enough," a voice commanded, and she froze, her arm still raised. Behind her stood her father, the Elf-King, in all his terrible magnificence. I could see now that his countenance was young and old at the same time, with all the beauty of youth and all the weariness and dissipation of age. His eyes were fathomless, pools of deepest green that had seen the passing of eons. When I looked at him, I knew with all my heart that I was looking at a great danger, and yet I could sense that even such a creature loved his daughter. He gazed at me as he had before, and this time I held his eyes with mine.

"You are free," he said in a musing tone, "and yet you remain. How very strange."

I gathered my courage and spoke. "We will not leave without Kai."

"The boy?" the Elf-King asked. "But my daughter wants him." He smiled indulgently at her.

"Is there . . ." I paused, thinking hard. "Is there nothing she wants more?"

The Elf-King's eyes widened, and I could see that

the question interested him.

"After all," I continued rashly, "he is human. He will grow old and die. Then she will have nothing."

The Elf-King's daughter, listening, pouted. "Father, can we not keep him young, like the changelings?"

"No, daughter," the Elf-King said in his silken voice. "He is already too old. He must wither and die."

The Elf-King's daughter stamped her foot petulantly. "But I want him to stay young, Father!"

"Is there anything you want more, my dear?" the Elf-King asked, echoing my words.

She thought, and I saw again the passage of time play across her face. Then her expression cleared, and she smiled happily.

"There is one thing," she said to me. "There is a jewel."

"A jewel?" I repeated stupidly.

"Oh, it is not just any jewel," she told me. "It is old, older even than our people, I have heard. It has great power. It is Odin's own cloak clasp, dropped as the Hunt passed by."

"But how do I get it?" I asked in a faltering tone. "Where is it?"

"It is in a palace not far from here," she said. "I can feel that it is there. When Odin dropped it, long ago, I looked for it; but it was already gone from the forest.

A boy had found it, and he hid it in the palace. I think of it there often. It calls to me, but of course we cannot leave here to get it. That is what I want. If you can bring the jewel to me, you can have this boy back." She motioned to Kai, who stood unmoving.

I looked at Karina, and she nodded.

"I shall bring it to you," I said. Then I added recklessly, "But I want the changelings as well."

I saw the Elf-King's lips narrow, and Karina's nails dug into my palm.

"You ask too much, girl," the Elf-King said in a deceptively mild tone. "Who would serve us then? And most of the families of those children are long gone. They were taken decades, centuries ago. To whom would they go?"

"I don't care!" I exclaimed. "I want Kai, and the changelings too."

"And I want the clasp," the Elf-King's daughter insisted. "Father, with it I could call Odin to me. He would have to come when I called! Wouldn't you like that?" Her tone was coaxing. "You would have that power over him then. And it is very pretty and would look well on my own cloak."

The Elf-King thought for a moment. Then he smiled tenderly at his daughter. "Beloved child," he said, "you know I can deny you nothing. It shall be as you desire."

To me he said, "Bring me Odin's clasp from the palace of Dalir, and you shall have your friend, and the changelings as well."

"Do you swear it?" I persisted. "Do you swear on . . . on Odin himself?"

The Elf-King's brows drew together in anger, and I stepped back, suddenly terrified. I was sure that I would be struck down by some terrible elvish magic. Whatever had made me ask him to swear?

But the Elf-King's daughter said, "Oh, swear it, Father! You know the clasp is worth it. Why, we will be stronger than Odin himself with it! Or so the stories say. It will be amusing to find out, will it not?" She laid a soft hand on her father's arm, and I could see him growing calm again.

"Very well," he said at last. "On Odin himself I swear it. The clasp for the boy and the changelings. However, I will grant you only a fortnight to bring the clasp here—a fortnight in human time. And the boy must stay with us until you bring it."

"Oh!" Karina cried in dismay. I knew she wanted to protest, but I also knew we had no choice. We had to leave Kai there, and we had only two weeks to find Odin's clasp. We had pushed the Elf-King as far as we could—much further than I would have thought possible, had I dared to consider it beforehand. We had a chance now, and we must take it.

"Come," I said to Ove. But he did not follow. Instead, he cocked his head, looking from me to Kai and back again.

"Very well," I said gently. "You can stay and protect Kai." I petted him, hoping that this was the right thing to do.

I began backing away, pulling Karina with me. Before we had gone far, I stopped and spoke again.

"From whom did you take me, sir?" I asked the Elf-King.

He turned once more to us, and I could see the question play across his face as he searched his ancient memory for the answer. But he did not reply. Instead he began to laugh; and his courtiers, his daughter, and her ladies laughed with him as they disappeared into the trees, gone in an instant, as if they had never existed.

6

A TRUE PRINCESS
DOES NOT GOSSIP

Karina and I turned then and fled. We both wept as we ran, aghast that we'd had to leave Kai and Ove in the thrall of the Elf-King's daughter. Before long, though, we had to slow to catch our breath, and finally we halted, unsure of what direction to take. I looked around wildly and spied a flash of scarlet that I was certain was not a redbird—for when had we seen or heard any bird but the falcon in that dreadful place? I was sure it was our nisse.

We started out again, trying to catch up with the nisse, but he hurried on ahead of us. When we slowed, he slowed too; and when we stopped to drink at a stream, he stopped as well. We tried walking in another direction, and he just stood where he was, waiting for us to turn back.

At last I lost patience. "Go around to the left," I instructed Karina, "and I will go to the right." As the nisse tried to follow our movements, we circled him and turned back, then stood before him, hands on hips.

"Well," I said. "What are you doing here? Why haven't you returned to the farm?"

The nisse adjusted his cap and smoothed his long beard. Then he shrugged. "The farm, the people—who's to say which needed me more? And you have given me treats. I like treats."

I smiled, remembering the scraps of food I had left out for him. "So you've decided to guard us?"

"To guide you," the nisse corrected me irritably. "Out of the forest. You humans are too stupid to get through on your own. Wolves, elves—it's hard to believe you've come this far."

"But what if the Elf-King catches you?" I asked. "Does he know you freed us?"

The nisse shrugged again, but I could see that he looked a little uneasy. "He'll probably have forgotten that by now. He's lived so long that he remembers only the most important things. And you are my people. It's my duty to keep you safe, much as I'd rather not."

"Well, thank you," I told him. "We are very grateful for your help. . . . Wait, do you have a name?" No one I knew had ever found out a nisse's name.

The nisse scowled. "Of course I have a name. What a ridiculous question."

"Well, what is it?" I asked.

The nisse gave me a scornful look. "That, missy, is none of your business. Now, are we going to walk, or would you like to stand here until the wolves come to eat you?"

We quickly gathered up our belongings and set out again. After a short while, the nisse held up his hand and said, "Listen."

We listened. Faintly, far in the distance, I could hear hoofbeats. Excited, I asked, "Is it the road? Are we near the end of the forest?"

"Stupid girl!" the nisse snorted. "Listen."

We listened again. The hoofbeats were closer, and we could hear the baying of hounds. Nearer and nearer, louder and louder the hoofbeats rang, and now sounded a horn so deep and loud that it seemed to rattle the trees and shake the very ground we stood upon.

Swiftly the nisse turned and ran until he found a copse of trees standing close together, and we followed him. He urged us into the center of the thicket. "Sit, cover your ears and eyes, and do not look, no matter what," he warned us. We crouched together and pulled our cloaks over our eyes.

"But what is it?" I whispered before I put my hands over my ears.

"It is Odin's Hunt, of course," the nisse replied shortly. "Now be quiet—and do not look!"

I fought the overpowering urge to look. I do not know whether it was the magic of the Hunt that tugged at me, or whether it was simply being told we could not look that made me long to uncover my eyes. As the Hunt came ever closer, the sound of the horn called to me, even through my hands pressed hard against my ears. *Join us!* it seemed to sing, and the hounds bayed, *Join us! Join us!* as the riders thundered past. I squeezed my eyes shut and huddled against Karina as the ground beneath us shook. On and on it went, and I tried to guess how many riders, how many horses and hounds made up the Hunt. Dozens, scores, a hundred?

At last the sounds faded into the distance, and we dared to uncover our ears and push back our hoods. I opened my eyes to see the nisse sitting cross-legged beside us, puffing on his long-stemmed pipe.

"Odin's Hunt," I said with apprehension, remembering what we had heard from the lords we had met at the inn. "Does this mean we are going to die?"

"You didn't look, did you?" the nisse asked. We shook our heads. "Then you'll live, most likely. But there will be a change."

I remembered the blue lord's words—*ah, then everything was changed*—and the terrible sadness in his voice. "What kind of change?" I asked uneasily.

"Oh, stop your chattering," the nisse snapped, his moment of patience over. He tapped out his pipe and rose. "Come along. We're almost there."

Almost there! The words galvanized us, and we jumped up as well, eager to find the end of Bitra Forest. I looked around as we left the thicket and saw that there were no hoofprints, no disturbance in the dirt, no sign at all that Odin's Hunt had passed by.

We followed the nisse, and as we did the trees gradually began to thin. At first it was barely noticeable, but then the air became a little brighter, a little fresher. I saw a shaft of sunlight fall to the ground and we moved faster, pushing through underbrush. Finally, we saw an end to it. The trees simply stopped. Beyond them stretched a green field sprinkled with flowers, and far in the distance were snow-tipped peaks: the Hamarr Mountains that I had heard marked the far edge of the North Kingdoms.

We stood at the edge of the wood, oddly reluctant to move from the trees and onto the field. After having been so long sheltered under the giant evergreens, we felt we would be unprotected, too visible, without them. As we paused, unwilling to start across the field, the nisse bowed extravagantly and tipped his red cap to us. Then he turned and walked back into the forest. We stared after him in consternation.

"Wait!" I called at last. "Where are you going?"

The nisse turned back, rolling his eyes at the question. "Home," he replied curtly.

"But . . . where do we go next?" Karina pleaded.

"That depends. Where do you want to go?"

"To the palace of Dalir," I replied.

The nisse pointed straight ahead, across the field. "That way," he said. "It's in Gilsa Town."

"Well," Karina said, "we are very grateful to you for your aid. Are you sure you won't go on with us?"

"Now, why would I do that?" the nisse snapped. "You're safely out of the forest, and I'm needed at the farm. Who's to know what damage has been done since I left?"

Karina nodded thoughtfully. "Yes, I am sure they need you there. Do take care of Father. And the baby, when it comes. And . . ." I wondered if she was going to ask the nisse to care for Ylva, but even Karina could not be that forgiving. "And thank you," she finished. She took a step forward and seemed about to hug him, and the look of utter panic on his face was too much for me. I snorted with laughter. The nisse glared at me, and before I knew it—*thump!*—I was flat on my back in the pine needles, the wind knocked out of me. By the time I could breathe again and had struggled to my feet, the nisse was long gone. Karina could not help laughing.

"At least he didn't set me on my head," I grumbled, brushing pine needles from my sleeves. "Good riddance!"

"Oh," Karina said, "he wasn't really that bad. A bit short-tempered, but really very generous."

Despite myself, I had to agree. "And," she added, looking rather pleased, "while you were lying in the dirt, he told me his name."

"Oh, what is it? Tell!" I begged. But Karina shook her head, mischief flashing in her eyes.

"I'll never tell, never!" she vowed. "I promised him I wouldn't."

"If I guess, will you tell?" I beseeched her, and she nodded.

"Is it Rumpelstiltskin?" I joked, and she laughed again, though I could see the shadow of her brother's absence in her face. To amuse her then, I guessed every strange or silly name I could as we left the gloom of Bitra Forest and walked out into the sun-warmed light of day.

On the far side of the field, we could see the road, and on it were travelers. We reached it quickly and strode along, glad for its even surface. I soon noticed that the people we passed looked at us rather doubtfully. I had not set eyes on a mirror for ages, but I saw Karina's face and knew that mine must be just as grimy, my hair just as tangled.

"We must look a fright," I said to Karina, and she nodded, trying to comb her fingers through her knotted blond curls. It was a wonder that the travelers did not run from us in alarm.

The road branched and branched again, gathering more travelers with each split, but we kept straight on. I saw traders go by with laden carts, and merchants riding fine horses, so I knew we were near Gilsa. At last we stepped through the oaken gates and onto the cobblestones of the bustling, well-ordered town. The houses were stone and strongly built to withstand the long, harsh winters, and there were shops selling wares of all sorts. We saw tailors and cobblers, fishmongers and butchers, furriers and barrel makers. There was even a sign maker's shop, to provide brightly painted signs for all the other shops.

When we passed a bathhouse, I said to Karina, "Before we go to the palace, we must clean ourselves up. They will not let us in looking as we do."

"But what shall we do when we get to the palace?" Karina asked anxiously. "We can't just go in and start looking in drawers and cupboards for a jeweled clasp."

"Nor can we ask about it," I agreed. "I have been thinking that we should try to get work there. As servants, we'll be able to look about freely."

"And what if the clasp is with the royal jewels?" Karina moaned. "Whatever will we do then?"

"We shall steal it," I said firmly, and her eyes widened at the thought; but then she nodded.

"For Kai," she reminded herself, pushing open the bathhouse door.

Once inside, we peeled off our filthy dresses; then we scrubbed and scrubbed until our skin glowed, and washed each other's hair until it squeaked. We washed our clothes and put on the one clean dress each of us had left in our packs. I felt like a new creature entirely when I was dressed, and I could tell Karina felt the same.

Bathed and refreshed, we set out for the castle. We had not gone far before we saw two of the lords we had met at the inn coming toward us. Karina nudged me in surprise as they approached.

"Ladies," Sir Erlend said, and we curtsied. He extended a hand to help me rise as the taller knight did the same for Karina. "We are glad to see you in Gilsa, out of harm's way. Often on our journey we spoke of you and worried about your safety."

Karina seemed quite tongue-tied, so I replied. "We arrived safely, sir, in part because of your friend's generosity. Without his sword, we all might have been lost."

"So the sword was used!" Sir Erlend said with great interest, and I proceeded to tell the story of our encounter with the brigands. The lords praised Kai thoroughly for his courage, but then Sir Erlend asked, "And where *is* your brave companion?"

"We have had to leave him in Bitra Forest," I said unhappily. "He looked on the Elf-King's daughter; and as you warned, the elves have taken him."

Karina bent her head as tears began to fall. The knights grew very anxious then, one offering an embroidered kerchief, the other moving uneasily from foot to foot. Like the men I knew—Jorgen and Kai— these two could not bear to see a woman cry.

Sir Erlend said at last, "I am very sorry. Sir Ivar and I would put our swords at your service on Kai's behalf, but it would do no good. The swords of humans have no strength against the elves there."

"That is why," the tall knight, Sir Ivar, told us, "the changelings taken from Gilsa are never recovered."

"So there have been many taken," I said, thinking of

the children at the elvish feast.

"Many indeed," Sir Ivar agreed sadly. "They wander into the forest—for the elves cannot come out, you see. They have as little power here as we have there. Even the royal family has lost a child, though that was long ago."

"How terrible," I breathed. Then, because I knew Karina would not ask it herself, I said, "And your other friend—the owner of the sword—is he in Gilsa as well?"

The lords exchanged a glance. "Ah," said Sir Ivar, "he has . . . other responsibilities. But I am sure he will regret missing the opportunity to see you ladies again." He nodded to Karina as he said this, and she blushed deeply, lowering her eyes.

"Please give him our regards," I said, to cover Karina's embarrassment. "And thank him for the sword. We are greatly in his debt, the more so because we can't return his weapon. The elves have it now."

"Our friend will understand," Sir Ivar assured me.

I gave him a grateful look and said, "If you'll excuse us, we are on our way to the castle to find work."

"Ask for Agna there, and tell her I have sent you," Sir Erlend said. "She will not deny you employment."

With that, Karina and I thanked him and took our leave.

We walked through the winding streets up a hill to the palace, which perched atop the town like an extravagant hat. Made of blue-tinted stone, its ornate turrets flew deep blue flags. As the breeze unfurled the flags, I saw they were decorated with stars and moons, and I thought suddenly of the blue lord's cloak. Could he be a courtier in the palace?

At the servants' entrance we were stopped by a guard, who told us to wait in the entryway for the housekeeper. We sat uneasily, smoothing our clothes and hair and inspecting each other's faces for dirt. After nearly an hour, the housekeeper, Agna, a no-nonsense woman with graying braids wrapped around her head and dark, keen eyes, marched up to us and asked sharply where we were from and what we could do. At the mention of Sir Erlend, though, she softened. It was plain to see that he was a great favorite of hers, and without further ado we were hired as chambermaids.

Karina and I followed Agna up many flights of stairs, past the bustling kitchen and pantries and the staterooms and the royal family's floor until we reached the top of the palace, under the eaves, where the servants slept. The room was empty at this time of day. Tall windows lined two of the walls, and there were numerous beds, each with a small wooden table beside it. Karina and I stared at each other, trying to imagine a household that required so many maids to run it.

Agna interpreted our look correctly. "There's as many manservants," she stated, "and the cook and I, and the butler as well. And the gardeners, of course, and the stableboys, and the herdsmen. This is a palace, girls, not a sheep farm in the country!" But she said it kindly, to put us at our ease. She pointed out the two beds that would be ours, and I was pleased to see that mine was nearest the door, so I could come and go at night when I couldn't sleep. It would make my search for Odin's clasp easier to have that freedom.

"Settle yourselves," Agna advised, "and then come down to the kitchen. There is a midday meal where you can meet the others. After that I'll explain your duties, and you can begin this afternoon."

She left us, and we unpacked our meager belongings, hanging our still-damp dresses in the common closet. I stroked the blanket at the bottom of my pack and pushed the pack to the back of the closet, behind the rows of shoes and boots. Then, without exchanging a word, Karina and I quickly searched the room, looking under beds, in the drawers of each bedside table, even in the pockets of the clothes in the closet. There was no sign of any finery, let alone a jeweled clasp.

"We'll find it elsewhere," I told Karina as we neatened our braids, smoothed our skirts, and brushed the

dust from our boots. Then we descended the servants'
stair to the kitchen. It was a cheerful place, with a blaz-
ing fire that was too warm, on this summer day, to
stand near. The cook, Elke, was a stout woman with red
cheeks and a loud, jolly laugh. Kelda and Griet were
her helpers, both about my age; and they served us soup
and bread at the long kitchen table. There were four
upstairs maids—Hulda, Janna, Petrine, and Birgit—all
welcoming enough. The manservants were too many
for me to keep straight that first day, but they seemed
friendly. Several of them made a point of speaking to
Karina. Her golden hair and blue eyes stood out in the
crowd of dark-haired, dark-eyed people, though there
was one man, Kettil, with bright red hair.

"From the east," whispered Janna when she saw us
looking at him. "I have my eye on him!"

"And what of you?" Birgit asked Karina. "You look
of an age to marry. Have you a husband in mind?"

Karina blushed crimson, and I laughed and teased
her. "Karina loves a handsome lord, but we do not
know where he lives, or even his name."

"Lilia, stop!" Karina protested sharply, and I looked
at her, surprised.

"Oh, a mystery!" Birgit cried. "Tell us about him."

Karina shook her head and would say only, "He is
very gentle, and very kind."

"He sounds lovely," sighed Janna. "Will you see him again, do you think?"

"He is so far above me in rank," Karina said softly. "Even if we were to meet again, nothing could come of it." Her voice was sad as she said this, and I rose to her defense.

"You are the equal of any lord," I said fiercely. "If he did not want you because of your birth, he would not be worthy of you."

"You never know," Birgit mused. "Perhaps you have a little royal blood in you. All the girls for miles around are hoping that is true of them, so they can pass the test and marry our Prince Tycho!"

"Oh, the test," I said, recalling the traders' discussion of it in the inn. It seemed so long ago now—when Kai was still with us. "What exactly is it?"

She shrugged. "No one knows. The girls come to the palace, stay a day and a night, and go home again. None of them will say what happens, but none of them has been chosen for the prince. It must be that they are not true princesses."

"But how do you know if they are or not?" I asked.

Birgit shook her head. "There must be a way to tell, I am sure. I have this." And she pulled from her pocket a little pamphlet and held it out to me. It was titled *How to Tell a True Princess*, written in very florid script. I opened it and read. *A princess's birth and upbringing instill in her the desire to behave in a way befitting her rank. She does not call attention to herself, nor does she engage in behavior unbecoming to a refined lady.* Below that I saw a list of rules. The first item stated, *A True Princess Does Not Eavesdrop.* Immediately I felt the heat rise in my face as I remembered sitting below the farmhouse window in Hagi listening to Ylva and Jorgen as they talked about me. I skimmed the rest. *A True Princess Does Not Perform in Public. A True Princess Does Not Gossip. A True Princess Does Not Travel Unattended.* Reading over my shoulder, Karina giggled.

"I suppose we might as well not try the test!" she whispered to me. I folded the pamphlet closed.

"Where did you get this?" I asked Birgit, handing it back to her.

"In town, at the bookseller's," she replied.

"The bookseller probably wrote it," I remarked. "Or his daughter did, longing to be a princess herself!"

The maids laughed.

"It seems a foolish thing, to make a bride pass a test to prove she is worthy of the prince," I said.

Birgit nodded. "They say the prince does not want to take a wife, but the king and queen insist on it. He turned down every princess they suggested, for this reason or that—one's nose was too long, another had hair too thin, a third did not converse with ease. And then they devised the test."

"But why?" I asked. "Why would he not want to marry?"

"Perhaps," Janna suggested, a faraway look on her face, "he is waiting for true love."

And with that Agna entered the kitchen. Birgit stuffed the pamphlet back into her pocket, and she and the other maids finished their meal quickly and scurried off.

Agna told us to attend to the staterooms on the floor above. "Stay away from the throne room," she warned us. "The prince will be holding audiences all day. We clean that room while the royal family dines—though it will just be the prince tonight, as King Ulrik and Queen Viveca are away."

We mounted the stairs one flight and hurried down the long hall, awed by the marble floors, the paintings on the walls of pale noblemen and ladies with dark hair and violet eyes, the gilded vases bearing heavy, drooping white peonies and vivid red roses. Everything looked already spotless to me, but I ran my feather duster over each surface, fearful of missing a speck of dirt and facing the kind of wrath I had once heard daily from Ylva.

"Oh, look at this," Karina exclaimed when we entered the ballroom, admiring its smooth parquet floor and cushioned window seats.

"I can just imagine an orchestra playing and ladies resting beneath the windows, tired and hot from the dance," I replied dreamily. Then I roused myself to lift the seat cushions and search beneath.

Next was the state dining room. We dusted the enormous mahogany table and each of the two dozen carved wooden chairs that lined it. When we were sure no one was looking, we rummaged through the drawers of the serving tables that lined the walls. We dusted and searched every room we entered but found no jeweled clasp.

At the end of that hall we came to a round reception room lined with curved benches. In the center of the room was a fountain that splashed water musically onto colored pebbles below. I was astonished that a fountain could bubble up endlessly indoors. Hot and tired, I dipped my hand in the cool water of the fountain, and Karina did the same.

When I turned, drying my hand on my apron, I noticed there was someone standing at the doorway. Fearful that we had been discovered doing something we ought not, I dropped automatically into a curtsy, lowering my eyes. Karina, also curtsying, gripped my arm tightly. I thought she'd lost her balance, but her hold did not loosen as we rose. I looked up then and saw, to my great surprise, the gentleman we had met at the inn, the man I thought of as the blue lord. He was dressed in blue again, a dark doublet of rich material. I was right—he was a courtier at the palace!

He came toward us, bowed, and said, "So we meet again." At the inn his courteous manners had seemed admirable; but here, in a palace, it felt wrong to me that he should bow so graciously to two serving maids.

"My friends told me they had seen you in town," he went on. "I am very glad that you made your journey safely—and that my sword proved serviceable."

Karina was speechless with embarrassment and shyness, so I replied, rather more saucily than I intended, "Indeed, sir, not as glad as we were!"

He laughed, and at once I felt more at ease. "But I am very sorry to hear of the plight of your companion. Will you tell me what happened?" He motioned us to one of the curved benches that lined the room.

"My lord, we cannot," I protested, thinking of the rooms we had yet to search. "We have work we must finish."

"I see," he said, noting our aprons and dusters. "But at least you could tell me your names, could you not?"

"I'm Lilia," I told him, "and this is Karina." Again we curtsied. As if we were ladies, he raised us gently, each of his hands holding one of ours.

"I am very pleased to make your acquaintance," he said formally, and then he said something that shocked me to my core: "I am Tycho."

I heard Karina gasp as he bowed over her hand, brushing it with his lips in a courtier's kiss. But this was no mere courtier—I had been gravely mistaken. This was Prince Tycho, son of the king, the heir apparent of Dalir.

The prince turned and left the room, and Karina and I stared after him wordlessly. Our faces were mirror images of dismay and astonishment as the sound of his boot heels clicked away from us, down the hall and out of earshot.

7

A True Princess
Faints When Frightened

Karina was silent and humiliated as we finished our dusting and left the round room.
"We had no way of knowing that he was
the prince," I tried to reassure her as we
descended the stairs to the kitchen for supper. "He
wore no crown."

"But his bearing was regal, and his manners were as
well," she said. "I am such a fool! How could I think—
how could I possibly imagine . . ."

She shook her head, and her eyes filled with tears.
I had known she liked the blue lord, known that she
thought he was handsome, known that she dreamed of
seeing him again; but until that moment, I had not fully

realized that she cared so much for him. Something in me rose up, and I said fiercely, "What I said before was right. If he feels he is too good for you, he is not worthy of you."

Again Karina shook her head. "He is a prince, Lilia," she reminded me softly.

"Ah, so you've seen our prince!" Birgit had overheard us and was eager to join in our conversation. "He is the most handsome prince in all the North Kingdoms—or indeed in any other kingdom that I know!"

Karina stiffened, and I spoke to cover her silence. "And yet he will not marry," I said.

"That he will not," Janna said, joining us. "He has created a test that no one who is not a princess can pass—but he has already refused to marry any princess in the North! Those who come now hope the test will reveal some unknown royal blood in their lineage, but it does not seem likely to happen."

"So does he not want to marry at all, then?" I asked.

"Our prince is a great mystery," Janna said fondly. "But he keeps things interesting with his test. In fact, we are to expect another hopeful bride tomorrow."

"Poor thing!" said Birgit, laughing, and the others laughed with her.

That night, I could hear Karina's muffled sobs in the bed next to mine. I reached out and took her hand in the dark, and held it until she relaxed into sleep. Then when everyone's breathing was deep and regular, I slipped on my dress and crept out of the room to continue my search for the jewel. Kai was never far from my thoughts.

The palace was lighted with candles placed here and there, and many tall windows welcomed the moonlight that was bright enough to cast shadows on the marble floors. I tiptoed through the kitchen, looking everywhere I could think of for the jeweled cloak clasp. The pantries were groaning with food: meats hung from hooks to age, and jars of lingonberry and cloudberry preserves lined the shelves. I saw barrels of flour and wine and baskets of nuts and grains. But there was no clasp.

There was a guard on the floor with the staterooms, but I slipped by him and entered the reception room with its gently plashing fountain. I saw that the blue tiles that lined the fountain were decorated with the same pattern of moon and stars that was displayed on the palace flags and Prince Tycho's cloak. The curved benches too were upholstered in dark blue velvet and embroidered with silver stars. I sat on one, tempted to stretch out on its soft cushions, but I feared being caught where I was not supposed to be.

The other staterooms were large and empty, a little

ghostly in the moonlight. I searched through them quickly, for Karina and I had looked in most of them once already. I entered the throne room, which we had not dusted, and marveled at the great carved throne where the king would sit and the smaller one at its side that I surmised must be the queen's. There was no jeweled pin beneath their embroidered seats or anywhere else I looked. Then I came to the last room on that hall, and to my surprise it was locked. I recalled that it had been locked in the daytime too—Karina and I had not been able to dust there. I resolved to ask the serving maids what it held.

At last I went back up the servants' stair, very tired but familiar now with the layout of the palace. I had crossed many rooms off my mental list of places to search. I slipped back into my narrow, lumpy bed without rousing anyone, and tossed and turned and dozed until daybreak.

In the morning, our second day since leaving the forest, the hopeful bride arrived. She came with an entourage of servants and her father, a plump, self-important merchant from the neighboring North Kingdom of Enga, to the west. They brought several wagons filled with trunks that we assumed held the daughter's dresses.

"Does she plan to stay for a month?" asked Hulda.

"Perhaps she has brought her trousseau," giggled Griet. "Does she not know that she will be gone in a day?"

I felt sorry for the girl, Ludovica, whose upturned nose and round, pink cheeks reminded me just a little of a pig. Though I knew that Karina wished her gone, neither of us joined in the mockery or the speculation that raged for the entire time Ludovica was at the palace. It was obvious that she was not of royal blood. Her manners were appalling. The kitchen buzzed with the news that she had curtsied very awkwardly when meeting the prince, scolded her maid publicly, and blown her nose in company. Griet and Janna were quite unkind about the way her bodice strained at its lacings, for she took after her father in figure. She ate like her father, too, Birgit noted after serving at table when Ludovica, her father, and the prince dined together.

"Three helpings of roast, and two of pudding!" she exclaimed, scandalized.

Karina replied, "It is a fine thing to have a good appetite. It means she is healthy." Birgit looked a little abashed at her gentle words, but Griet snorted and said, "Healthy indeed! Healthy as a cow at her cud!"

After dinner and an evening of awkward talk—reported by Janna, who brought in tea—I watched discreetly as Agna led Ludovica to the room at the end of the hall. The housekeeper unlocked the door and went in with Ludovica, and a few moments later she came out again, locking the door firmly behind her. There was no chance for me to see anything. I was oddly frustrated. The room seemed to call to me; I felt I *must* see what was inside.

The next morning, Ludovica emerged bright-eyed and rested. During breakfast—at which she reportedly ate plate after plate piled with lacy pancakes filled with preserves, pulla rolls spread with sweet cheese, and sausages—the prince took her aside, and they exchanged words that no one was able to overhear. The discussion was enough to send Ludovica weeping to her room. Not long afterward, with her face veiled to disguise the signs of tears from onlookers, she left the palace with her father and their vast retinue.

"But how did she fail?" I asked the maids. "Did she eat too much, or speak too little?" They shrugged; no one knew, and no one had been able to find out.

I realized that I would have to wait to see inside the room until the next eager bride came, for it was locked again and the key well guarded by Agna. At the first opportunity, I waylaid Birgit, the friendliest of the maids, and asked her what the room contained.

"I have never been inside," she admitted. "I believe it was once a music room, but now it must be a bedchamber of some sort, for the girls who come to win the prince sleep there. I tried to peer in once, and Agna nearly had my head!" She laughed, and I smiled distractedly. Her words made me hopeful that the room might hold what I was seeking, and I was determined to look within. Each hour that passed made me more apprehensive, more fearful for Kai's safety in the forest. The two weeks the Elf-King had granted us were slipping away.

Though I could not get into the locked room, I continued my search. I did not stop with the palace interior, but extended my hunt out-of-doors. At our first free hour, Karina and I headed for the gardens, which were enormous and well tended, with flowers, bushes, and herbs of all sorts planted in intricate designs. At one end there was a wilder patch of garden, with a beautiful weeping cherry tree. The tree was ancient, its branches bending gracefully to the ground so thickly that it created a little cave. Surely a jewel could be hidden in there!

We crawled inside the branch cave and breathed deeply of the cherry-scented air. I searched every inch of the tree and the ground around it but found nothing more than fallen cherries.

"Kai would love this tree," Karina murmured. "Remember how fond he is of cherries?"

I nodded, plucked a ripe fruit, and popped it in my mouth. She followed suit.

"Do you also remember what he and I would do with the pits?" I asked mischievously, and I spat my cherry pit at her.

It smacked her on the shoulder, and she returned the assault, leaving a mark on my apron. Back and forth the cherry pits flew. One of mine had far too much breath behind it and sailed past Karina, landing with a *splat* on a face that had just ducked inside the branches.

It was Prince Tycho's face.

I stared, horrified, at the red smear the cherry pit had left on the prince's cheek. Karina turned and let out a moan of embarrassment. But the prince started to laugh, and he laughed so hard that he had to lie down on the grass under the tree and hold his stomach.

"I am so sorry, Your Highness," I said when I could bring myself to speak. "I never meant—"

"You are a powerful spitter," Prince Tycho gasped. "Are you as deadly with an olive pit?"

I started laughing then too, and even Karina had to join in. The prince ate a cherry himself and aimed the pit at a branch, and we made a game of it. Before long, my mouth was tired from spitting, my stomach hurt from laughter and an excess of cherries, and I was sure that I was smeared with cherry juice, as Karina was.

On her it looked very fetching, though, staining her lips a bright crimson.

"I must go back," I said at last. "Agna wanted me to polish the silver."

"I'll go as well," Karina said, but the prince protested.

"No, stay and keep me company. Now that you have discovered my favorite hideaway, you should enjoy it with me."

"Oh—oh, Your Highness—," Karina stammered, flustered.

"Tycho," the prince said. "That is my name. Under the weeping cherry, we must not be formal."

Karina, her eyes downcast, did not reply.

"Please stay," the prince pleaded. "Just for a bit."

I took a deep breath and said, "You're not needed until supper, Karina." I wasn't sure if leaving her was the right thing to do, but something about the prince struck me as trustworthy. The look Karina gave me was both terrified and grateful, and I crept out of the cherry cave, anxiously hoping that my impulse was not a mistake.

That night Karina told me about their conversation under the tree. "He offered to go to the forest to find Kai," she said.

"But Sir Erlend said it would be useless to try," I pointed out.

"I know," she said sadly. "And the prince agrees that this is true. But he offered nonetheless."

"That is very noble."

"Lilia, perhaps we should tell him—you know. About the clasp. And why we are here."

I shook my head. "Don't you think it would sound strange, that we are looking for a jewel? Surely he would think we have come to rob him."

"Oh no, he would never think that!" Karina protested, but she sounded uncertain.

"If I don't find it in the locked room, then you can tell him," I said. "Just give me another day or two. A new hopeful bride is coming the day after tomorrow. I plan to get in right after she leaves."

"I will go with you," Karina said decisively.

We were quiet for a moment. Then I asked, "Was that all that happened under the tree?"

"He read me a poem that he had been working on," she told me.

"Was it good?" I asked.

"I liked it very much," she said shyly. "You might not have. It was a ballad about a brigand, like the ones we met. He said we were its inspiration."

"Ah," I said knowingly. "And was there a lovely golden-haired lady in it?"

Karina laughed, very quietly. "Well, yes," she admitted.

"She was threatened by the brigand and rescued by the hero. It rhymed quite beautifully."

"And did the hero marry the lady at the end?"

There was a silence. "The poem was unfinished," Karina said softly. Then she turned over in her bed and went to sleep.

Later that night, I returned to the cherry tree hoping to sleep, for my restless nights in the maids' chamber and my relentless search had left me exhausted. I dozed on and off, waking at dawn to see a group of courtiers ranging over the hillside. I crawled out from my hiding place, recognizing Sir Erlend and Sir Ivar among them. In the center of the group was Prince Tycho, and on his gloved arm rested a falcon, smaller than the one I had seen in Bitra Forest but huge nonetheless. The prince carried the bird with great authority. It was hooded, and when the men reached the hill's highest point, the prince pulled off the hood and called out loudly, jerking his arm upward. The bird started and rose from the prince's arm, its great wings beating steadily, the bells that hung from its leather jesses tinkling. It flew so high that I could barely see it.

Then came another shout, and the bird began to descend. It came like an arrow, and none could see where it aimed at first. It seemed that it was headed not at a rabbit in the field or a game bird on the wing, but straight at me. I stood up, bewildered, as the bird plunged toward me. I saw its curved beak and sharp talons, but I did not duck or try to hide or even flinch. I am sure the hunters watched with horror, and I could hear them calling faintly, but I had eyes only for the falcon. Truly, I was not afraid. And at the last possible moment the bird pulled up, beating its wings hard to slow and stop itself, and settled on my shoulder as gently as a leaf falling from a tree.

I looked at the bird, and it—or she, for I knew somehow it was a female—tilted her head and looked back at me. She had the same knowing gaze as the falcon in Bitra Forest. I bowed my head as I had to that bird and said, "If you helped me when I was a baby, I thank you." And she bowed her head back at me, the bells on her jesses jingling, exactly as if she understood every word.

Then the hunters ran up, and all was confusion for some moments. The falcon found her way back onto the prince's arm, and Sir Erlend's hands were on my shoulders as he asked insistently, "Are you hurt anywhere? Did the bird do you harm?"

I shook my head. "No, milord," I said firmly. "I am fine."

Prince Tycho whistled gently, and the falcon's head tilted in a listening pose. "I have never seen the like," he said. "This bird has never flown for another. I trained her myself. She has never perched on anyone else's arm."

I smiled at him. "I think falcons like me, Your Highness," I said. "She is not the first one I have known."

"You are surpassing brave, lady," said Sir Ivar admiringly. "The way you stood your ground as the bird came at you—most ladies would have fled screaming, or fainted dead away."

"Most men as well," the prince said, and the hunters laughed.

"I am not much for fainting," I said. "But I don't know if it was bravery that caused me to stand still. Some would call it stupidity." I smiled again, thinking of the nisse. To be sure, he would call me stupid!

"Not at all," insisted Sir Ivar gallantly. "We salute you, lady, and your courage." And to my astonishment, the hunters, every one, took off their caps and swept me a bow. I curtsied in return, pleased beyond measure. I had never been accused of bravery before, and it felt very satisfying indeed.

Sir Ivar offered to accompany me back to the palace, but I was acutely aware of the gossip this would cause, so I politely declined. There was gossip nonetheless; the story of my encounter with the falcon raced through the palace and grew with each retelling. By the time it reached Karina, I had been torn nearly to bits and required the strength of six courtiers to be rescued from the bird's vicious attack. She burst into the queen's bedroom where I was dusting in preparation for the king and queen's return—and looking for the cloak clasp—her face panicked and as pale as bleached wool.

"I am *fine*," I assured her before she could speak.

"But whatever happened?"

I calmed her with the truth, but it made me uneasy to see how wistful she looked each time I mentioned the prince in my telling. Her feelings for him had clearly deepened.

That evening as we undressed for bed, I winced as I eased my dress over my head, and I heard Karina gasp when the fabric pulled free of my shoulder. The other maids gathered around me. I looked in the glass, shocked into silence at the sight of six small, deep holes in the front of my shoulder, and two in the back, all crusted with dried blood: imprints from the talons of the falcon.

8

A TRUE PRINCESS DOES NOT STEAL

By the next day, I was tired of correcting the endless variations on the story of my encounter with the falcon and just let it grow as it would. The maids gossiped freely about my wounds, which Karina cleaned and bandaged, and the manservants treated me with a grudging admiration. In addition, Sir Erlend, Sir Ivar, and the other courtiers began acknowledging me more openly when we met. While they did not bow as they would to a lady, they did nod their heads or tip their hats. Of course, this fueled the gossip. I had gone from Lilia, the country shepherdess, to Lilia, the brave survivor of an attack by an enraged bird of prey (version the first) or

Lilia, the girl who could tame wild birds with a single word (version the second). I found, rather to my surprise, that I did not much mind the attention or the newfound respect. Whenever I began to believe in my own marvelousness a little too much, though, Karina and Agna were at hand to bring me back to reality. Karina would remind me of how I used to fall asleep over the washing-up, and Agna would hand me a dust cloth, an apron, and a list of wearisome chores.

The next wishful bride was to come that day, and I laid out my plan.

"Give me one of your hairpins," I told Karina. "After she has gone home, when everyone is asleep, I will pick the lock and sneak inside."

Karina looked thoughtful. "It could work," she allowed. "But if you are caught . . ."

"I know where all the guards are, and when they make their rounds," I said. "There is no danger."

Karina nodded decisively. "Good. We have taken far too long looking for the clasp already. We haven't much time left!"

Edda arrived as scheduled. She was not at all like the porcine Ludovica. She traveled with her mother, a reasonable number of servants, and only one small trunk. She was rather pretty, with exotically high cheekbones and luminous hazel eyes.

I could see that she made Karina very anxious.

"She is beautiful, is she not?" Karina whispered to me.

"Merely attractive," I protested. "And that red hair—it is like unpolished copper, not at all as nice as blond hair." But that was a lie, and we both knew it.

"She will be gone by tomorrow," I reminded Karina.

"Oh, I do hope so," she breathed.

That evening King Ulrik and Queen Viveca returned from their progression through the uplands. A good deal of pomp and celebration attended their homecoming. All the staff was required to come out as the carriages arrived and curtsy or bow in unison. We were at a fair distance from the king and queen, but I observed their imperial stature and graceful movements; the king's dark hair and beard, streaked with gray; the queen's fair skin and downcast eyes. They looked exactly as I imagined a king and queen should look. They hurried into the palace with their attendants and servants, and we scattered to prepare for an elaborate meal. Edda and her mother would join the royal family and their court at dinner.

"The queen seems rather solemn," I remarked to Janna as we laid the long table in the state dining room.

"Yes, she has always been thus," Janna told me. "She rarely smiles, though she is a queen and has a fine husband and son."

"Why is that?" I asked, adjusting the space between water and wine goblets.

"I don't know why. Ask Agna—she's been here forever. She knows everything," Janna said.

"I shall," I replied. "Now, are all the forks and knives in the right places?" There were five of each. I could hardly imagine a meal that would require so many utensils, but later I watched amazed as course after course left the kitchen, each more pleasing to the eye and nose than the last. It very nearly rivaled the Elf-King's feast, and it made me think all the more of Kai, and of the captive children who had served that terrible meal. Moved by a growing sense of urgency, I decided to change my plan and try to sneak in and search the room while Edda slept. I did not share this strategy with Karina, for I knew it was very possible that I would be caught, and I did not want to involve her.

"She is doing very well," Griet, who was serving, reported about Edda. "She uses the correct forks and has not spilled anything. She is conversing with some spirit. The prince is even smiling at her."

After the meal, the diners retired to the royal sitting room, where Edda played the harpsichord and sang in what Griet described as a "passable" voice. At last, the king and queen and prince bade good night to Edda and her mother. I watched as Agna took the mother to one of the guest chambers on the floor where the royal family slept. Then she descended to the floor below with Edda. I followed cautiously as they walked down the long hallway and stopped at the locked door. Again, as she had with Ludovica, Agna unlocked the door and entered with Edda; again she emerged a few minutes later, locking the door behind her. I smiled to myself as I touched Karina's hairpin in the pocket of my apron.

Late that night, I snuck downstairs again and made my way silently to the chamber door. I was about to use the hairpin on the lock when I heard a noise from inside. I listened carefully. It sounded like Edda was pacing back and forth, back and forth. I sat down on the marble floor to wait for the creak of the bed frame, for the silence of sleep, but the pacing continued until I began to feel drowsy. I knew that I must leave or I would fall asleep and be discovered—and what would Agna say then? Exasperated, I made my way back up to the maids' chamber, where I dozed fitfully in a straight chair until dawn.

In the morning we could hear even from the maids' room that the household was in an uproar. Karina and

I dressed quickly and rushed to the kitchen with hair unbraided to find out what had happened.

"I don't know exactly," the cook, Elke, admitted as she rolled lacy pancakes around lingonberry preserves. "They are saying that she may have passed the test."

Passed the test! I glanced swiftly at Karina and saw that her eyes had filled with tears. "We shall find out the truth," I said, taking her hand. We found Agna in the hallway outside the kitchen. "What is it?" I asked her. "Has Edda passed the test?"

Agna pursed her lips. "It is not for me to say," she said shortly. "She may have. The prince will decide."

"Do you know what the test is?" I pressed, but she only shook her head at me, whether to say *No, I do not know* or *Stop bothering me* I could not tell.

"Go do something with your hair," she ordered us, and I put my hand to my head, remembering that we had left our locks unbraided.

As we ran upstairs to our room, forgetting to take the servants' stair in our hurry, the prince was coming down. He halted when he saw us. His eyes were on Karina, and I turned to see what had caused him to stop and stare. Her golden hair cascaded over her shoulders untamed, and the color was high in her cheeks as she returned his look. Their exchange lasted only a brief moment; then he bowed his head and continued past us, and we made our way, more slowly now, to the maids' chamber.

My hair braided, I left Karina upstairs and skimmed back down the main stairs just as Edda was passing by with her mother on their way to breakfast. Her face was pale and her eyes shadowed; she looked as if she had not slept all night. I recalled her endless pacing in the room.

"I was so nervous," I heard her whisper to her mother. "I could not lie in bed at all—I did not even try. I have trod miles this night!"

"My poor child," her mother said soothingly. "We will make an early evening of it. You will sleep all the better tonight. Now pinch your cheeks to put a little color in them. It's time to greet the prince."

Edda did not leave that morning, but there was no proclamation that she had passed the test, no announcement of her engagement to Prince Tycho. Instead she spent the day with the royal family, hunting with the falcons and dining again in the state dining room. The gathering did break up early, and it was a good thing, as Griet told us, because Edda's exhaustion was evident. Her manner was less lively, and she was too tired to sing.

By the next morning most of the staff had managed to position themselves so they could see Edda when she emerged from the bedchamber. Agna frowned at us and sent us scurrying as she came to bring Edda to breakfast, but Karina and I moved as slowly as we could and were able to observe her as she appeared, her hazel eyes clear and bright. Karina sagged at the sight; but when I looked at Agna, I saw a secret smile on her face, though I knew not why.

After the morning meal, Prince Tycho took the red-haired beauty aside and spoke privately to her. His words had no visible effect; but with her head high, Edda instructed her servants to pack. An hour later she and her mother departed, seemingly unaware of the curious stares of staff and courtiers alike.

"Well," said Hulda, watching them leave, "if that one cannot pass the test, nobody can. The prince will go to his grave a bachelor."

In the afternoon, Karina found me and reminded me that we had to sneak into the locked chamber that night, though of course I had not forgotten. I could hardly wait for night, I was so excited. I was somehow certain that we would find the jewel there.

But that night, all our plans came to nothing. In the early evening another lady arrived, unannounced and unexpected. This one, Idony by name, was from the South Kingdoms, much farther south than Hagi. She traveled with a small retinue: a maid and two guards.

She was very beautiful. Her hair was silver and fell to her waist in shimmering waves, and her eyes were a clear gray-blue. Her mouth was full and rosy, her alabaster skin flawless. The king, queen, and prince received her graciously; and belowstairs we quickly threw together as festive a dinner as we could on such short notice. Birgit served, and she reported to us as we sat at our supper in the kitchen.

"She is as bright and sparkling as a diamond," she said. "The king and queen seem entranced by her. She has spoken about poetry and politics—it is obvious that she is well educated."

"And the prince—is he entranced as well?" I asked, for Karina's sake. I knew she would not ask herself.

"He seems to like her well enough," Birgit replied. "He smiles quite sweetly at her, and she has made him laugh twice."

Karina pressed her leg against mine under the table, but I did not dare look at her. I felt terrible.

All evening we snuck looks at Idony whenever we could, passing by the dining room, where she sat radiant and self-possessed at the long table, or later wandering past the sitting room, where she sang a duet at the harpsichord with the prince. He had quite a nice voice, and hers was high and sweet. They blended beautifully, but the tears in my eyes as I listened were not for the harmony of their song. *He belongs to Karina!* I thought fiercely.

The night passed like the others when ladies had come to stay. Agna took Idony to the chamber, led her in, and left her. All that night Karina was as wakeful as I. We served at breakfast, bleary-eyed but anxious to learn of Idony's fate.

Idony looked much as Edda had after her first night. Her gray eyes were deeply shadowed, and her face was drawn with fatigue.

"Did you sleep well?" the queen asked as they took their seats. When Idony shook her head, I saw the queen grow very still.

"Your Majesty, perhaps I was nervous; but I could not sleep a wink all night, though the bed was soft," Idony admitted. "I tossed and turned as if I lay on bare ground."

I nudged Karina to pass the tray of jams and jellies as the queen placed her hand on Idony's.

"Oh, my dear," the queen breathed. At her tone, my heart seemed to stop beating. The queen turned to the king and Prince Tycho, seated to her left and opposite her at the table.

"My son," she said softly. "Here is your bride."

I was bewildered. What had Idony done? How had she proved she was of royal blood? I looked at Prince

Tycho and saw that his face had gone white. The king, beside him, smiled broadly.

"We are so pleased—," the king began, but Prince Tycho interrupted him.

"Forgive me, Father, Mother," he said. "I cannot allow this to continue. I am so sorry, Princess Idony, but I cannot marry you."

Karina's mouth dropped open. To her credit, Idony reacted as a true princess would. She smiled graciously and said, "You do not have to ask for forgiveness, Your Highness." Then, shockingly, she went on, "I cannot marry you either. I am the one who should apologize."

"Why should you apologize, milady?" King Ulrik asked. His voice was mild, but his eyes, when he looked at his son, flashed fire.

Princess Idony blushed and looked down at the table, twisting her napkin in her hands. "It was not my idea to come here," she admitted. "My parents, the king and queen of Asar, insisted on it. They knew I would pass whatever test you offered, for I am a true princess; and they long to see me married to a prince. But you see, I am in love with a man who is not my equal—or so *they* say." She said the words softly, but it was clear that she was hurt and angry.

"Not your equal?" Prince Tycho echoed with great interest. "Is he a commoner, then?"

"He is a nobleman, but only a knight," Princess Idony said. "Still, he is the best, the bravest and truest man I have ever known. I mean no offense, milord."

Prince Tycho smiled. "None taken, milady."

"I did not want to come," Idony went on. "I am sorry to have taken advantage of your hospitality, but I never intended to marry you. How could I? My heart belongs to another."

I let out the breath I hadn't known I was holding, and I saw my relief mirrored on Prince Tycho's face. *He does love Karina!* I realized with a thrill. *He truly does!*

"But what will you do?" Prince Tycho asked Idony.

"I will return to my home, and I will tell my parents that either I marry my beloved or I marry no one at all. I am their only heir. Though I hate to hurt them, I think they will accept it."

Prince Tycho rose and came around the table. He took Princess Idony's hand in his and raised it to his lips. "I wish you the best, milady," he said. "It is a lucky man who wins you."

Princess Idony turned her brilliant smile on him. "And I wish you well too, milord," she replied warmly. "I feel I have found a friend here today—and I think our situations are not so different." I alone saw the prince glance at Karina when she said those words. Then the princess stood and curtsied, Prince Tycho bowed, and she left the room to instruct her maid to begin packing her belongings.

As soon as she was gone, King Ulrik turned to his son, his face taut with anger. Sensing a gathering storm, the queen quickly waved us from the room. We did not go far, though, but positioned ourselves at the slightly opened door and eavesdropped shamelessly, peeking inside when we dared.

"Well, sir," the king began. "Would you care to explain this to us?"

Prince Tycho sighed and returned to his seat at the table. "I have no real explanation, no excuse," he said at last. "I know that I agreed to the test, but it was never my true intention to wed anyone who passed it."

"What are you saying?" the king thundered. Again Karina's mouth dropped open in astonishment.

"I am sorry, Father," Prince Tycho said uncomfortably. "But I agreed to the test only to give me time."

"Time for what?" the queen asked.

"Time to . . . oh, Mother, I don't know! Time to learn my own heart, I suppose."

"My son," Queen Viveca said, "do you love another? Is that why you would not marry any of the princesses we suggested?"

"I—I cannot say, Mother," the prince said miserably. "All I know is that I cannot marry anyone I do not love."

I stole a glance at Karina, who looked quite overcome with the prince's declaration.

"Forgive me, Father, Mother," the prince begged. "I
will not deceive you again."

"But you must marry!" the king insisted. "This
ridiculous talk of love must end right now!"

"Oh, Ulrik," the queen said gently, rising and going
to him. She laid a hand on his sleeve, and he looked up
at her. "My dear, how can you speak of love as ridiculous? Were we not in love when we married? Do we not
still love each other? How could we have endured our
terrible sorrow without our love to sustain us? Surely
you would not wish a loveless marriage on our son."

The king looked long at his lady, and his face softened. "No," he said at last. "No, of course I would not.
I can see that I have been foolish. It is only that . . .
there has long been a hole in our family. I thought perhaps that a daughter-in-law could fill it."

"I know," Queen Viveca whispered, and the king
stood and put his arms around her. Suddenly I wished
I were elsewhere, and Karina and I backed silently away
from the doorway.

Once safely down the hall, we turned to each other.

"What happened in there?" Karina asked me. "Did
the prince really—was she—"

"I believe so," I said. "I believe that the lady Idony

somehow proved herself a princess, and that she refused the prince. Or he refused her. Or both!" We began to laugh, and Karina clasped her hands together.

"I think he loves only you," I told her. "I'm certain that is what he could not say to the king and queen."

"Naught can come of it," she said sadly, sighing with both pleasure and pain.

"I don't know," I said. "Princess Idony's tale may have given him hope—and courage. If she is brave enough to stand up to her parents for love, perhaps the prince will follow suit."

"But the princess's beloved is a knight," Karina pointed out. "And I am but a shepherdess."

"Stop that!" I cried. "You are the bravest, most beautiful girl in the world! In fact, I think you are too good for Prince Tycho. How dare he hesitate to name you as his love?"

Karina tried to cover my mouth, as I had spoken quite loudly, but I ducked away from her. "Oh, hush, Lilia!" she begged. "Someone might hear. He is not afraid on his own account, but on mine. He does not want me banished, sent home to Hagi in disgrace. It is not as simple as you think it."

I put my hand over hers. "I can see that," I said more calmly. "But I hope he finds his way soon, for I cannot bear to see you suffer so."

"At least there will be no more hopeful brides," Karina said, and we laughed halfheartedly.

"If the test is over, we may never learn what it was," I mused. "But we still must get into the bedchamber, for it is the only place Odin's jewel might yet be. We have to try tonight—we have only six days left to find the jewel and bring it back to Bitra Forest."

That night we waited until our bedroom was filled with the gentle sighs of maids sleeping. Then we dressed swiftly and crept out, down the servants' stair to the second floor. After a quick check to make sure the way was clear, we scurried to the chamber. Silently I picked the lock—a skill I had not been sure I possessed—and the door eased open. We slipped inside.

Long windows let in enough moonlight to see the interior, and we looked around, prepared to be astounded by grand opulence. But to our shock, the room was bare—completely empty but for a bed in the center. And what a bed it was! It was canopied with embroidered velvet swags in deepest blue, and its coverlet too was sapphire velvet, embellished with the familiar silver stars and moon. Lace pillows lay in heaps upon it, and a lace bedskirt swept the floor. The lofty mattress was so high that a little stair with three steps stood beside it to enable a sleeper to climb up.

We circled the bed and looked under it, but the

wooden floor was as clean and bare as the walls. There was not a picture nor a tapestry for a jewel to hide behind. There was only the magnificent bed, like an ornate ship afloat on a wooden sea.

"How very peculiar," I observed, my voice echoing off the uncovered walls.

"Shhh!" Karina cautioned, a finger to her lips.

I whispered now. "There is nothing in this room that could hide the jeweled clasp, Karina."

Karina's face mirrored my own dismay. If the clasp was not here, where could it be? And if we could not find the clasp, how could we rescue Kai? We had looked everywhere, in every nook and cranny of a palace filled with nooks and crannies. I could not imagine where else we could search. The only room left held the crown jewels, and it was guarded by two soldiers at all times. It seemed impossible that we could get inside without being caught. And somehow I did not feel that Odin's clasp was there.

"We should go," Karina said sorrowfully.

"Wait," I said suddenly. "What about the bed?" We lifted the heavy mattress as far as we could and peered under it. Then I pointed to the piles of pillows and heaps of bedclothes. "Under the coverings!" I exclaimed. Karina nodded decisively, and climbed the stairs onto the bed.

"Oooh," she sighed. "It is the best bed in the world. Come up, Lilia!"

I climbed up too and jumped onto the mattress, bouncing Karina. I pulled aside the pillows, seeing nothing beneath them, and looked under the blankets—again, nothing. I glanced at Karina, wondering why she did not help me, and saw to my surprise that her eyes were closed, her breathing soft and regular. She was fast asleep! How could she sleep at a time like this?

But then the bed enveloped me, almost as if it were alive. *Sleep*, it seemed to say. *How can you not sleep on me?*

I feared that I would join Karina in slumber, and I fought against it. After a moment, though, I began to realize that the mattress was not as soft as it first appeared. In fact, under its surface, it was surprisingly lumpy. I could not get comfortable, and I found that I was no longer in any danger of falling asleep. Quite the opposite, in fact—I knew that even if I had wanted to, I would not have been able to sleep on that bed. I tried to wake Karina, but I could not rouse her.

I looked around the empty room again. In the moonlight the chamber seemed strangely familiar, and I climbed down the stairs to examine it more closely. I put my hand on the wall, searching for something—I could not say what—and then I noticed that there was a little indentation in the wood. I pushed in with my fingers; and to my shock there was a creak, and a little door popped open in the wall near my feet. My instinct had been right!

The door was no more than waist high, so I knelt down and crawled inside. I found myself in a tiny room, hardly more than a closet. Like the chamber, this little space was empty, but for one thing. In the center sat a box, inlaid with mother-of-pearl. Breathless, I sat and stared at the box for several seconds before I picked it up and carried it out of the little room so I could see it more clearly. It was heavy in my hand. Even before I opened it, I knew. On a bed of deep blue velvet lay what I had been seeking for so long: Odin's cloak clasp. *At last!* I thought. *Kai will be saved!*

The clasp was made of white gold and had been wrought by an artist with skills far beyond those of humans—that was clear. The gold was twisted into intricate vines and leaves and flowers, with jewels that I did not recognize set at the flowers' hearts. The colors of the jewels seemed to change as I looked, from green to blue to violet. It was the most beautiful thing I had ever seen. I turned it over and over in my hand before I slipped it into the pocket of my apron. Then I closed the empty box and put it back in the little room, crept out again, and shut the door. It latched with a muffled *click*. I could not tell, looking at the wall, that the door had ever been there.

I tried to shake Karina awake to show her the clasp, but her sleep was still so deep that she did not stir. I whispered her name, then said it again, but still she slept on. I could see from the daylight outside the long windows that the palace would soon be awake, and I began to panic.

"Karina!" I said, and shook her again. "Karina, wake up! I've found it! We must go—come on, wake! We will be caught!" In my fear, my voice had grown very loud.

Without warning, there was a sudden crash. I turned as the door to the room flew open. My heart sank as I saw two guards, their eyes wide with shock at the sight of us in the forbidden chamber, and behind them, Agna's furious face.

9

A True Princess Is Not Contradictory

hat are you doing in here?" Agna
demanded. Then her glance fell on
Karina, still sleeping soundly in the
great bed. Her expression grew even
more enraged, if that was possible; and she marched
over to the bed, climbed the stairs to the high mattress,
and shook Karina, much harder than I had.

"What? What is it?" Karina gasped, shocked at last
out of her deep slumber. She sat up, blinking the sleep
from her eyes.

"Get down, girl!" Agna ordered. I had never seen
her like this before. She was strict, perhaps, but she
had always been even tempered.

Karina climbed down quickly and came to stand beside me. She was pale and kept her gaze on the floor, but I looked at Agna, trying to figure out just how angry she was.

"It was my fault," I began. "Karina did not—"

"You should not have done it," Agna said severely, interrupting me. "What were you thinking? Did you hope to prove you were princesses? Foolish girls!"

"No, Agna! How could we even do that?" I asked, confused. "There is nothing here to prove a princess. There is nothing here at all!"

Agna shook her head. "Foolish, foolish girls," she repeated. To Karina she said sarcastically, "You slept well, I assume?"

Shamefaced, Karina nodded.

"And I see that you did not even get up on the bed," she said harshly, turning to me.

"Well—well, I did," I admitted. "I climbed up with Karina, but the bed was lumpy. I could not sleep. But I can never sleep in a bed, so it was . . ." My voice trailed off into what seemed a great silence. Agna was staring at me with a look I could not interpret at all. Astonishment, suspicion, disbelief, even fear seemed at war upon her features. Finally she said, "You lay on the bed but did not sleep?"

I nodded my head, bewildered.

Agna was silent, chewing on her lower lip. Then she said abruptly, "Come with me, both of you." She turned toward the door, and we scurried behind her. Down the hall and up the stairs we rushed, to the sitting room. The empty room was pretty and comfortable, with cushioned chairs and thick carpets. Small tables held vases of fresh flowers. It was so cheerful a place that I allowed myself to hope that nothing truly bad could happen to us there.

"Sit," Agna said, pointing to a small loveseat. We perched on the edge, our backs straight, trying to look as if we were too well bred to have done anything wrong.

"You will have to wait here," Agna told us sternly. "The king and queen are holding audiences today. Their schedule is very busy. I do not know when they will be able to see you."

We nodded humbly, and Agna left us.

"The king and queen!" Karina exclaimed as soon as the housekeeper was gone. "If we are going to be dismissed, why must the king and queen be involved?"

I shook my head. "I don't know. It makes no sense to me." Then I remembered. "But Karina! I found the clasp!" I reached into my pocket and pulled it out.

Karina stared in amazement at the clasp. She reached out to touch it, then snatched her hand back as if it had given her a shock.

"Oh, Kai is saved," she whispered. "You have done it, Lilia!" She looked more closely at the jewels. "It is beautiful. Where was it?"

"In a tiny hidden room, behind the wall," I said. "Somehow I felt that it was there—and I was right. But we must get back to the forest with it straightaway. We are almost out of time." I rose and walked to the door. It was locked, and I rattled the knob in frustration. "We are trapped here! How can we escape?" I ranged around the room, looking out the windows, but they were too high above the ground.

Karina said, "We will tell them, when they come to us. I know Prince Tycho will understand. They will let us go."

"Are you so sure? How do you know?" I asked.

She looked down at her fingers interlaced on her lap. "The prince has asked me for my hand," she said in a near whisper.

I stared at her, astonished. "He has proposed to you? Karina! When did this happen? What did you tell him?"

"It happened just after the princess Idony left. I told him no, of course," she replied. "How could it come to pass—a prince marrying a shepherdess? His parents would never accept me as his wife. His people would never accept me as their queen."

I took her hand in both of mine. "You are mistaken," I said. "They would love you. Who could not love you?"

"I am not mistaken," she said, her tone sad but very firm, and we spoke of it no more.

Before long Agna returned and stood to one side as King Ulrik and Queen Viveca swept into the room. Prince Tycho followed them, and when his gaze fell on Karina, I could see his concern. We stood quickly and curtsied.

"So, Karina and—Lilia, is it?" the king began. His voice was deep and measured, and he did not sound angry.

"Yes, Your Majesty," I breathed.

"You took it into your heads to see if you could pass the test, is that right?" the king asked.

I risked a look at Karina and saw that she appeared as bewildered as I felt.

"N-no, Your Majesty," I stammered. "We just—we only wanted to see what was in the locked room."

Then, to our shock, the king laughed. "So," he boomed, "you did not even know what the test was!"

"No, Your Majesty," I whispered. "No one knows."

"I will tell you first that you could not have passed. I am sure you are not surprised," the king told us.

"Father!" Prince Tycho protested, though whether he objected to his father's tone or to his words was unclear to me.

I could not help asking then. "But what is the test, Your Majesty? The room was completely empty but for the bed."

Prince Tycho came forward and stood near Karina, but she did not raise her eyes to him. "The bed *is* the test," he told us. "Perhaps you know that royalty can sleep only on royal beds, for we have a certain . . . well, a sensitivity that makes it impossible for us to rest on ordinary surfaces, no matter how soft they seem to others."

I shook my head. I had not known that.

"Well, the bed in that chamber is a royal bed, so ordinarily any royal person could sleep on it. And this bed, in fact, has had its comfort a little enhanced, so not sleeping is impossible for someone without royal blood."

"Enhanced?" I repeated, intrigued.

"A little magic was applied. There is a—a person in Gilsa who can do such things," the prince explained. "But there is more." He took an object from his pocket and showed it to me.

"It is . . . a dried pea?" I asked, confused.

"Yes, a pea. This was sewn into the mattress. A truly

royal person would feel it as if she were lying on a stone. She would not be able to sleep at all, despite the magic."

There was silence in the room, and I darted a glance at Agna. She stared straight at me, her mouth pursed.

"You—you did not tell them?" I asked her. Agna shook her head.

"Tell us what?" demanded King Ulrik.

Finally Karina spoke. Her voice was low and calm, but her words had the effect of a whirlwind passing through the room.

"I fell asleep instantly, but Lilia did not. The bed was too uncomfortable for her."

The king's eyebrows shot up and Queen Viveca gasped, her hand covering her mouth. I could see that although her skin was nearly as smooth as porcelain, there were faint lines on her face that hinted at deep sadness. She seemed familiar to me, and I suddenly realized that she resembled the woman who often appeared in my dreams, the beautiful lady who moved so gracefully but whose features I never saw.

The queen came forward to me then and reached out for my hands.

"My dear," she said in a voice as clear as a bell, "you are a true princess. The test cannot be wrong. If you could not sleep on that bed, you must be of royal blood."

I felt strange and dizzy. "Oh, but it must be wrong!" I cried. "I am no princess; I am a serving maid! The pamphlet—*How to Tell a True Princess*—everything it says a true princess does, I do not. I am just a maid, and a shepherdess before that. Oh, Your Majesty, I cannot be a princess!"

The queen felt me tremble and led me to the loveseat. "Sit," she said, and sat beside me, still holding my hands. "There is no guide to telling a true princess," she told me gently. "The only real test is the bed."

I shook my head wildly but could not speak. "Who are your family?" Queen Viveca asked me. "We can soon learn whence your royal blood has come."

I was silent.

"Child, where do you come from? Who are your people?" she persisted, looking at me intently.

My palms grew damp and clammy, my eyes filled with tears, and I choked out the words: "I do not know." I looked down at the floor, willing myself not to cry.

Behind me I heard Karina explain, "She came to us as an infant, floating down the river in a basket. She has never known any family but mine. She is my sister, as truly as Kai is my brother." I loved Karina completely for that, but still I could not look up, afraid that my tears would spill over.

"In a basket?" the prince repeated.

"Well, it was not really a basket. We thought it was, but now we believe it was a falcon's nest."

"What a tale!" Prince Tycho marveled. "A princess in a falcon's nest—'tis the stuff of legends!"

I listened to this exchange as if it were taking place in another room, in another life. I felt detached from everything. It was all unreal and absurd. Through the film of my tears, I pulled my hands from the queen's, stood, and went to the window, where I looked out and into the distance.

As I stared, almost unseeing, I began to notice something very strange. The horizon, where it met the mountain peaks, had turned from the deep blue of early evening to green, and it was pulsing lightly. I watched as the green color moved upward and shaded into teal, then inky blue, blue-purple, violet, lavender. The whole sky now was bathed in vivid colors, and it pulsed like the world's heartbeat. Astonished, I remembered the dream I'd had weeks before, on the day I left the farm. The sky in my dream had looked just like this.

"Oh," I said faintly. I felt my own heart throbbing in time with the wild sky, and I turned back to the room, my eyes wide.

Prince Tycho looked out the window to see what had startled me. "Those are the Northern Lights, the aurora borealis," he said.

"Those are the colors of my dream," I said wonderingly. "And the colors of my blanket."

The silence in the room was as loud as a scream, and I saw Queen Viveca's pale cheeks grow whiter still.

"Your blanket? What blanket?" she asked in a voice that thrummed like a harp string tuned too tightly. She stood, holding herself very still, as if she was afraid she might fall to pieces if she moved.

Karina spoke up again. "She was wrapped in a blanket when my father found her. She has the blanket still."

"Show us," the king demanded. I moved to the door, and Agna opened it for me. Outside, in the hall, Griet, Janna, and Hulda were busily dusting objects that did not need dusting, and they circled me as I made for the staircase.

"Lilia, what happened? Are you dismissed? What did they say?" they asked me; but I barely heard their words. I pushed by them and stumbled up the stairs to the maids' bedroom. I opened the closet door and scrabbled for my pack, which was behind the shoes and boots where I had left it. I pulled out the blanket, breathing in its scent. I almost believed that I could smell the bright breeze that blew in the meadow where Kai and I had watched the sheep in Hagi.

Cradling the blanket, I hurried to the sitting room. No one had moved since I had left.

The queen came to me slowly, holding out her arms for the blanket. When I gave it to her, she lifted it to her face, rubbing its softness on her cheek. Then she laid it across my shoulders and placed her hands on my cheeks, raising my face to hers so she could look deep into my eyes.

"Oh, my own baby, my own little girl," she breathed. "I thought you were taken for a changeling, my darling daughter. All these years I thought you were gone forever to the elves; but here you are, alive—alive and grown. This is the blanket that I wove for you. I would know it anywhere. You never let it out of your sight; and when the Elf-King took you, it disappeared with you."

I tried to speak, but only a little squeak came out. I remembered, dimly, the words Sir Ivar had spoken on the streets of Gilsa: *Even the royal family has lost a child, though that was long ago.* I had thought he meant generations ago, or that the child lost was a royal nephew or niece or second cousin. But could that royal child have been the daughter of the king and queen? Could I have been that child?

I gazed into the queen's eyes, which brimmed with tears—and they were my own eyes, the color of spring violets. The dizziness I had felt earlier came back, and suddenly it seemed that the exhaustion from an entire life of sleeplessness was pressing down on me. The room spun crazily around us as we stood together. I was not much for fainting, as I had said to Sir Ivar when the falcon landed on me, but I could not help closing my eyes and crumpling, most ungracefully, to the floor.

10

A True Princess
Does Not Travel Unattended

I think I was not unconscious for long. I opened my eyes to see the anxious faces of Karina, the king, the queen, and Prince Tycho as they bent over me. Someone had lifted me and carried me to the loveseat, and the blanket—my baby blanket—was placed over me. I clutched it with cold hands and tried to sit, but my head ached dreadfully.

"Lie still, Lilia," Karina said, her voice worried. "You've had a terrible shock."

A shock indeed! "So it is all true?" I said with a dry mouth. "It was not a dream?"

"No, not a dream," Karina replied. "All this time, my dear friend has been the princess of Dalir—the long-lost princess of the Northern Lights!"

I shook my head, and the room spun. "Surely you do not believe this, Karina! It cannot be true!"

The queen pulled up an embroidered hassock to sit beside me, spreading her wide skirts gracefully. "My dear child," she said gently, stroking my brow, "it does seem too strange to believe, but I rejoice that it is so."

The prince cleared his throat then, and spoke.

"Lilia—Sister," he began, and my heart jumped at the word. "I must tell you that it is my fault that you were lost to us."

"No, my son!" Queen Viveca protested. "It was not your failing. You were but a child!"

"I was eight, Mother, old enough to have known better," the prince said quietly. "You were nearly two, Lilia, new to walking and to speaking. We spent considerable time together. I took you out to view the falcons, and we loved to watch them hunt. We sat together at tournaments, and I held you high so you could see. I thought of myself as your protector." Now bitterness crept into his voice. The queen reached up to place a soft hand on his arm, and he went on.

"I wanted my way in all things, as young children do, and I was determined to ride with the hunt that fall. Father said I was too young. I begged, but he would not yield. Of course he was right; I could not even ride a full-sized horse, but I was furious. So I ran away. And to frighten Father, I took you with me."

Here he hesitated, and I saw that his face was tortured with remembering. I could recall nothing of this—or could I? All my life, I'd dreamed of the falcons, and of tournaments, of palaces and royalty. Could the things I had dreamed be memories from my childhood?

"I dirtied our faces and clothes so we would not be recognized," Prince Tycho continued. "We ran through town and across the fields to Bitra Forest. I'd heard warnings about the forest, but I thought as an eight-year-old does: *They will be sorry when they learn where I have gone!* And so we entered the forest. Almost immediately we were lost."

The room was hushed, waiting. Prince Tycho went to the window and looked out at the Northern Lights, flickering still. Then he turned to us and continued.

"I carried you for a time, but soon I grew tired, and we curled up by a giant fir tree. It was then that we heard the Hunt approaching."

I closed my eyes, remembering the terror of Odin's Hunt when I was in Bitra Forest with Karina.

"I knew the tales, so I covered you with my cloak and closed my eyes and stopped my ears as they passed. And we survived. But then came the promised change."

I recalled again the prince's words about the Hunt

when we had met him at the inn, when he was just the blue lord to me: *and after—ah, then everything was changed.*

"I was frightened then, and so very tired, and I sought to find my way out of the forest. I tried to make you walk, but you would not, so I carried you. And thus we passed by accident into the Elf-King's domain." Here the prince turned his back to us, and we had to strain to hear him.

"The elves surrounded us, and the Elf-King came forward. He said I was too old and he would not take me, but he held out his arms for you. I could not resist. I gave you to him. I gave you to him." His voice broke, and I realized that I was weeping too. I rose from the loveseat, my head clear now, and went to him and touched him lightly on the arm.

"I have seen the Elf-King," I told him. "You could not help it. You had to give me up. He cannot be disobeyed."

"But I was your protector," he whispered. "And I did not even try."

"If you had been a grown man in full armor with a company of knights at your side, you would have had to give me up," I said fiercely. "You had no choice, I promise you."

He turned to me and clasped my hands tightly. Then I asked, "When you heard the Hunters pass—did you find anything? Any remnant of the Hunt?"

Slowly he nodded his head. "Yes. How did you know? There was a pin—a jeweled cloak clasp. It lay on the ground, and you picked it up. I was afraid you would stick yourself, for it was very sharp. So I took it and put it in my pocket; and I did not think of it again until days later. And then—then you were gone, and I could not bear to remember. I hid it in a secret place where you and I once liked to play hide-and-seek."

"Is this the jewel?" I asked in a near whisper, pulling the cloak clasp from my apron pocket.

Tycho reached for it and held it for a moment. "How did you find it?" he asked me.

"I don't really know," I admitted. "Perhaps I remembered the hidden room from when we were small. I just seemed to know it was there."

The prince showed the clasp to the king and queen.

"It has been in the palace all these years, and we never knew," the king mused.

"I have never seen its like," Queen Viveca said. "It is not human made."

"I must bring it to the Elf-King," I told them then, taking the clasp back from Tycho, and they stared at me.

"But its owner is Odin—or one of his Huntsmen," Tycho said at last.

"It is Odin's own clasp, and I must give it to the Elf-King," I said again. "I have made a bargain with him. In return for the clasp, he will give me Karina's brother, Kai, and the changelings. I haven't much time. He gave me only a fortnight to find it, and well over a week has passed already. If I do not go, they will be lost forever."

"No!" the queen cried out. "You cannot go!"

"I must," I said simply.

Prince Tycho and his father exchanged a look. This was something they understood well; it was a matter of honor. "Then we shall all go," said the prince. "Ivar, and Erlend, and the others, and Father and I. With all our swords, surely we will be strong enough."

"But your swords have no strength in Bitra Forest," I reminded him.

"We can but try. You cannot go alone," the prince insisted.

"Indeed you cannot," King Ulrik echoed him. "We have just found you, my child. We will not lose you again."

"I would be glad of the company," I said falteringly. "I am . . . I am dreadfully afraid of the Elf-King."

"Oh, Tira!" the queen said in a trembling voice. I looked at her, confused.

"Why do you call me that?" I asked.

"'Tis your birth name, dearest," she replied. "It was my grandmother's name, and her grandmother's before her."

Of course. It had not occurred to me that I had once been given a name different from the one I now had. Jorgen had named me Lilia when he plucked me out of the river.

"I—I have been Lilia for as long as I can recall," I said hesitantly. "I don't know if I can take another name."

The queen looked down, distressed, and the lines around her mouth deepened. Immediately I wanted to call back my words.

"I will be Tira if you wish," I said. "I am sure I will become used to it."

"No," the queen said, raising her eyes. "You have earned the right to the name you want. Lilia is a lovely name, and I shall be proud to call you that." She smiled at me so sweetly that at last I began to believe it all, and I came forward into her embrace. Her arms were as tight and warm around me as my blanket had been, and I sank into them.

Then King Ulrik threw open the sitting-room doors and called for strong tea and food. Karina sat close to me and said, "I am coming as well."

I put my hand over hers and nodded wordlessly. But

the queen heard, and she said, "I too will go with you, Daughter."

Daughter! The word made my heart swell within me, and tears came to my eyes.

Agna brought in the tea, and I smiled at her apologetically as she served us. It felt very strange, and somehow wrong, to be served by her; but she appeared comfortable enough handing me my cup and bowing her head to me. We ate and drank quickly as Tycho went to gather his men.

When we were ready, the king—my father—led us out of the room, along the long hall, and down the marble steps. The men's swords rattled against their chain mail, and their boot heels rang on the floor. I wore my blanket like a shawl, for it gave me courage, and I kept my hand on the jeweled clasp in my pocket. The staff watched us silently as we left, and I wondered what wild stories would fly up to the eaves and back down to the kitchen after our departure.

Horses awaited us at the palace gates. I eyed them uneasily. I had never ridden a horse, only Jorgen's aged donkey. These animals seemed to rise halfway to the skies, and they stamped the ground with enormous hooves.

"You will ride with me," King Ulrik said softly, noting my nervousness. "Your brother will take Karina.

We shall camp just outside the forest, for night is coming on, and tomorrow we will find the Elf-King."

Then he swung me up onto the saddle of his horse, and I realized how fine it was to view the world from such a lofty perch. I could see everything! My father leaped up behind me, and his arms holding the reins held me secure as well. We set off, cantering down the hill to Gilsa and through the streets as the people waved at us and called out to the royal family. I thought once I heard a cry of "Princess Lilia!" but I assured myself that I was mistaken. Surely the townspeople could not know my story already—or could they? Perhaps gossip moved as quickly through the town as through the palace.

We reached the forest's edge just after nightfall. The knights quickly set up elegant tents, small but comfortable, with carpets on the floors and lanterns hanging from hooks inside, casting a warm light. There were cots to sleep upon and canvas chairs for sitting. I could hardly believe such an elaborate camp could be constructed in such a short time, but Karina pointed out that knights are trained in such things.

I was too nervous to eat the simple meal the knights handed out around the campfire, and Karina and I returned early to the tent we shared. Once inside, though, I found I could not sleep for worrying. What if I did not reach Kai in time? What would happen to him? I crept out again after Karina's breathing had eased into slumber and wandered about the encampment, close to the overarching trees of the dismal forest. I came to where the knights sat drinking mead and talking in low voices around the campfire. One by one they trailed off to their tents, and soon only Prince Tycho remained. I stepped out of the shadows, startling him.

"Lilia!" he said. "Please sit down." He motioned to the canvas stool that one of the knights had vacated, and I perched there.

The silence between us, broken only by the crackling of the fire, was awkward, so I forced myself to ask the question that had plagued me. "Do you truly believe you are my brother, Your Highness?"

He smiled at me. "Truly I do, Lilia. And so you must not call me 'Your Highness,' for you are 'Your Highness' too, and it would sound ridiculous."

I laughed and had to admit this was so.

"Do you really have no memory of your time with us, Sister?" Tycho asked me.

"I don't know," I said. "I have dreams of things that might have happened. And the queen—she seems so familiar, somehow. And I knew where to find the hidden room in the locked chamber. Could these be memories?"

"I think they are," Tycho replied decisively. "Memories that such a small child would have had, turned into dreams and feelings and impulses over time."

"When this is over . . ." I sighed, and shivered, thinking of the Elf-King. I pulled the blanket tighter around my shoulders.

Tycho noticed and said, "You are cold. You should go back and try to rest—though of course you will not sleep on a cot! No one has yet figured out how to make a cot that royalty can rest upon. None of us will sleep well tonight."

"But in the palace—," I said longingly.

"Ah, in the palace we will give you a bed that will make up for all your years of sleeplessness!" Tycho told me, laughing, and I laughed again too.

Then, a little embarrassed, I asked him another question that had been preying on me. "Brother"—the word sounded so strange!—"what of Karina?"

His face grew solemn. "Yes, Karina," he said sadly. "She will not have me, you know."

"I know," I replied. "She told me. She feels that the gap between you is too great, and that the people of Dalir would never accept her. She cannot bear that you would sacrifice yourself for her."

"She does not give my people enough credit," he

said. "Whom I love, they will love. And who could not love Karina?" My heart went out to my brother then, for the look in his eyes when he said that.

"Even our parents?" I asked.

"I can see that they are already fond of her," he replied. "How could they resist her? They know how good she has been to you—and I hope they will see how good she will be to me."

"Then you must ask her again!" I said impulsively, and he gave me a quick grin.

"Perhaps I will," he agreed. "Now rest. Dawn will be here soon."

The night was long for me, and I tossed and turned, waiting for daybreak. When it came, we assembled at the edge of the trees. Karina and Queen Viveca would stay at the camp; but they watched as the men, armored and on foot, gathered in formation. King Ulrik, Prince Tycho, and I were in the lead. I put my hand in my pocket, reassuring myself that I still had the cloak clasp.

Prince Tycho addressed his knights. "Princess Lilia and I have faced the Elf-King, and we know he is not to be trusted," he said in a firm voice. "It may be that we simply hand him the jewel and he hands us the children and Kai, as promised. But if not, we must be prepared."

The knights, ten in all, unsheathed and raised their swords as one. The blades caught and reflected the rising sun, and I thrilled to the men's courage.

"Let us go!" Prince Tycho called out, and we turned to march into the forest. I walked right in—but the prince did not. Instead, he staggered back as if he had walked into a glass wall, and the king and the knights behind him did the same. I stood just within the trees, and watched with horror as the knights attacked an invisible barrier that again and again repelled them. Karina ran up then, and she too was unable to enter. My mother pressed her hand against the barrier as if it were a window. On the other side, I put my hand up to press against hers, but I could not feel her touch and knew she could not feel mine.

I heard the others calling me to return, but I did not. I did not even know if I could leave, now that I was inside the forest, and I didn't want to find out. If I knew that I could escape, I might lose my courage. I had to find Kai and the changelings. I had to free them.

Slowly I backed into the woods, watching the faces of my friends and family, new and old, grow smaller and smaller. My parents' expressions were filled with worry and fear, and I ached to think of how they must feel, to lose their daughter to the forest twice. Then I turned away and began to walk, knowing I had to go south. I remembered when Kai and Karina and I had guided ourselves by the moss that grew on the north side of trees, so I headed away from the side of the trees on which the moss grew green.

I was hopelessly lost in minutes, but before I had time to panic I saw once more a familiar red cap, and our nisse popped up before me.

"Why aren't you at the farm?" I asked him, knowing better than to let my relief show in my voice.

"Why aren't you at the palace?" he retorted, and I smiled despite myself.

"I am glad you are here," I admitted, though I tried to keep my tone light. "I have to find the Elf-King, and I do not know where he is."

"So I understand," the nisse grumbled. I wondered how he knew, then realized that news doubtless traveled fast among magical folk. "What an idiot you are!" he went on. "It wasn't enough that you escaped the elves unharmed. Now you want to tempt the fates again—and you put me in harm's way as well. You know that you are my charge and I am bound to help you."

I shook my head. "I am no longer a shepherdess, it seems. You don't need to help me—I release you. I don't want to put you in danger. You can go back to the farm."

The nisse snorted. "I'd far rather help you than that dreadful fat farmwife you lived with. But you are alone. Where is the other one?"

I looked at him, and he made an elaborate show of looking away unconcernedly. I remembered how flustered he'd become when Karina had tried to hug him, and I hid another smile.

"Karina is waiting outside the forest. You can see her if—when—" I broke off.

"We might just go there now and save our lives instead," the nisse suggested.

"No," I said firmly. "I must rescue Kai and the changelings. I promised."

"*I promised!*" the nisse repeated, mocking me. "Is that why? Is that really why you risk your life—and mine?"

I looked closely at him, and saw a glimmer of understanding in his green eyes. "You know it is not the only reason," I said softly, and he rolled his eyes.

"You humans—you are all rotten with emotion. Can't you just be a princess and be happy?" he chided me, but he did not expect an answer.

He began walking, and I scrambled to follow him. Once again we walked and walked, though this march seemed to take far less time than when we were fleeing the elves. Before long we reached the clearing where the Midsummer's Eve feast had taken place. It was empty now, the grass lush and untrampled, as though a bonfire had never blazed and elvish feet had never danced there.

"Stand in the center and call him," the nisse instructed me. "But be wary. The Elf-King has little regard for promises made, and no regard at all for human life. I cannot help you once he comes; I can only watch."

I gulped. "If—if I do not come back, will you tell Karina what happened?" I asked, my voice trembling. "Will you tell her I tried my best?"

The nisse frowned, but he nodded. "I'll tell her," he promised. "Now go!"

I stepped forward into the clearing until I stood right in the center of it. Looking up, I could see a circle of blue sky far, far above. Then I took a deep breath and called out, "Elves, I am here! I am here for the Elf-King and his daughter!"

11

A True Princess
Does Not Consort
with Commoners

I stood in the clearing for several minutes, torn between dreading the appearance of the elves and fearing they would not come. I was sorely tempted to turn and run, but I made myself stay. I stayed for Kai.

And suddenly they were there, and I took a step backward, trembling. The Elf-King stood before me, with his golden crown and ageless eyes; and at his side was his lovely daughter, with her treacherous smile. Behind them were five elvish archers, holding their bows.

"You came back, Princess!" the Elf-King's daughter said gaily, her green dress rippling like tall grass as she moved toward me. *How,* I wondered, *has she discovered that I am a princess?* And then I realized that she had known all along, since the day I had first been taken from my brother. She had known, and kept it from me, and this made me angry. It was easier to be angry than afraid.

"I did come back," I replied grimly. "I see I am quite a danger to you. Do you truly need five archers to protect yourself from me?"

The Elf-King's daughter laughed, but this time I felt no inclination to laugh with her. "You are amusing," she said fondly. "They go where we go. We do not fear you, silly girl. Now, give me my jeweled clasp."

I took a deep breath. "First, I would like you to tell me something." A little line appeared between her brows, but she nodded gracefully. "I escaped from your father as an infant," I reminded her, as calmly as I could. "How did that happen?"

A look of puzzlement passed over her features. "So you did," she said. "Ah, now I remember! My father grew tired of your squalling. He gave you to a servant to hold, and then a falcon came."

"A falcon?" I said, confused.

"Such dreadful birds!" the Elf-King's daughter complained. "It fell from the sky like a stone and snatched you away from us. We did not even have time to draw an arrow. You were gone in an instant. Father knew it was revenge for what he had done so long before, when he shot a falcon for sport. Oh, how he raged! It was really quite entertaining." She glanced at the Elf-King, and her laughter pealed again. "We thought perhaps the bird ate you, or fed you to her chicks," she confided. "But when we saw you at Midsummer's Eve, we realized that was not the case."

"She placed me in her nest and floated me down the river," I told her. It was the last part of my story. Now I knew all.

"What an astonishing tale, and what a lucky girl you are!" the Elf-King's daughter said nonchalantly. "Now, where is the cloak clasp?"

I put my hand in my pocket and fingered the clasp. "Where is my friend?" I retorted. "And where are the changelings?"

Now the Elf-King spoke up, and his voice was commanding. "First, give us Odin's clasp."

My knees were weak, but I shook my head. "You may have the clasp when I have what I came for," I said firmly.

The Elf-King glowered at me, and I lost my breath. His face was as terrible in anger as it was beautiful in repose. "Give it to me!" he demanded, holding out his hand and moving toward me, his daughter following.

I struggled to breathe and gasped, "You—you promised!"

The Elf-King's daughter laughed yet again. "He is the Elf-King, and you are but a human," she said reprovingly. "What matters a promise between you two? Now, give us the jewel."

"On Odin himself you swore it!" I cried out. "You cannot break such an oath!"

The Elf-King and his daughter stopped in their tracks, and I could see that my words had perplexed them. I took advantage of their confusion to turn, intending to flee; but I heard the Elf-King say something in a strange tongue, and I turned back to see that the archers had raised their bows.

At that moment I heard a wild, high-pitched call. The elves heard it too, and their heads whipped around to find the source. Before they could pull their arrows to defend themselves, five falcons had plunged through the opening in the trees and were upon them. The great birds did not attack, though. As swift as a bolt of lightning and as unexpected, the falcons flashed by the five elves and were up in the air again a second later, each holding in its sharp claws a quiver full of arrows. In an instant they were gone.

Before the Elf-King and his daughter could recover from their surprise, I ran. Frantically I fled through the forest, dodging around trees, too afraid to look behind me to see if the elves were following. The nisse was suddenly beside me. "The clasp!" the nisse shouted. "Use the clasp!"

Then I remembered what the Elf-King's daughter had said when she first asked for the clasp. *With it I could call Odin to me.* I stopped running, pulled out the clasp, and held it up. I cried out, as loudly as I could, "Odin, come to me! I call you to me!"

Immediately I felt the ground shake beneath my feet, and I knew the invocation had worked. The Hunt was approaching. "Quick!" the nisse said. "Do you have something to bind your eyes?"

I felt in my other pocket and found a dusting cloth, left from what seemed like another lifetime, when I was just a serving maid. I fastened it around my head, covering my eyes.

"I must hide myself," I heard the nisse say as the sound of wild hooves came closer and closer. And then I was alone in the forest, blind, as the Hunt bore down on me.

I had thought that I'd felt fear before—when I defied the Elf-King and when I'd hidden in the copse as Odin's Hunt had passed me by. But this was beyond any terror I had ever known. I stood my ground as the Hunt raced toward me, knowing I could be crushed by the hooves of Odin's giant horse; and truly it was not courage that held me there. It was fright. I could feel the wind of the Hunters' movement as they came closer and closer—and then it stopped. All stopped. Time itself seemed to stop. The forest was utterly silent but for the sound of my own heart hammering in my ears.

Then Odin spoke, and his voice, like his horse's hooves, caused the earth to tremble.

"You have called me, human, and I have come."

I held up the cloak clasp, my hand shaking so hard I thought I surely would drop it. Again there was silence as I struggled to find my voice. At last I whispered, "I have your cloak clasp, milord."

"It has been missing a long time," Odin replied. "I had nearly forgotten it. Why is it in your hand?"

"It was found by my brother many years ago, and hidden all this time," I said in a very small voice. "I had promised it to the Elf-King."

"Why did you make that promise?" Odin inquired. "It was not yours to give."

I gulped. "I see that now, milord," I said humbly. "But promise I did, in return for the humans whom the Elf-King holds prisoner."

I heard the shifting of horses' hooves, and I wondered how many Hunters there were. I could feel them all about me, ringing me, though they did not touch me. The breath from their horses stirred my hair.

"And why is this my concern?" Odin asked me.

"The Elf-King swore an oath," I said. "He swore on your name. And he has broken his promise."

"Ahhh," Odin said, and the *ahhh* rumbled like an earthquake. The rumble went on and on, and I lost my balance and fell against a tree. I could feel the great trunk tremble as the ground heaved beneath me. I sank to my knees, still clutching the clasp.

Then I heard the horses shift, and I smelled a scent so sweet and exotic that it almost made me swoon. I knew it was the Elf-King's daughter, though I had not noticed her scent before, so caught up had I been in the sight of her. She smelled of lilac and wisteria and a spice I could not name, and with it was a whiff of evergreen that I surmised was her father. I longed to see them confronted by Odin, but I kept my hands securely at my sides, knowing that to uncover my eyes was to die.

"Milord," I heard the Elf-King say, his voice warm and affectionate. Still, beneath the warmth I thought I could detect something else. Worry, perhaps? Even fear?

"You vex me with trifles," Odin's low rumble came. "You know I do not like to be bothered when I hunt. And yet you have made it necessary for me to stop my Hunt and attend to you. What say you?"

Odin was speaking to him almost as a parent scolded a child. It was hard for me to picture the Elf-King so meek, but I found it pleasing to try.

"I do regret it greatly, milord," the Elf-King said, and now to me his voice sounded oily, groveling. "It was not my intention to disturb you, not at all. This is a matter between the human and myself. There is no need to trouble you with it."

"No need?" Odin growled, and again the earth trembled, just a bit. "You swore an oath on my name!"

"Yes. Well." Now the Elf-King seemed a little ill at ease, and my heart leaped with hope. "That will not happen again. The human—"

"The human fooled you, fool," Odin said, and I thought I heard the glimmer of a laugh in his voice. Then the horses moved again, and Odin, closer to me now, said, "Human, lay the clasp upon the ground. I cannot touch you."

I moved forward a little on my knees and felt the hot snuffling breath of a horse as it bent its head to sniff me. I placed the clasp gently on the ground and scuttled back against the tree.

"Father!" the petulant voice of the Elf-King's daughter rang out. "It is mine! Do not let him take it!"

"Be quiet, daughter!" the Elf-King warned, but it was too late.

"It is yours?" Odin said, and then louder, "It is *yours? Yours?*" The ground heaved violently once and I screamed despite myself, and the Elf-King's daughter screamed as well. I could picture her as she picked up her green skirts to run, as I would have done if I could, and I heard the patter of her feet as she fled. The Elf-King must have intended to go with her, for Odin called him back.

"Stay, Elf," he said. "You have not fulfilled your oath."

"Milord," the Elf-King replied, "I thought that since I did not get my prize, I did not have to pay for it." I marveled that he dared to say such a thing to Odin.

"You should not think so much," Odin remarked, and again I thought I detected a laugh behind the words. "Bring the human prisoners here when I have gone. Alive. All of them. Lift their enchantment, and let them go free."

There was a moment of silence, and I held my breath. Then, in a sulky voice that echoed his daughter's, the Elf-King said, "Very well, milord. As you command, so shall it be done."

"Wait!" I cried before I could stop myself. "I need something more."

"And what is that?" Odin asked. His tone was impatient now, but I persisted.

"I need safe passage for all of us out of the forest. I fear the Elf-King will kill us as we try to find our way."

"So he would," Odin said. "You are a brave one, human, and a smart one as well, to understand your enemy thus. Grant it, Elf."

I could almost feel the Elf-King's rage as he spat out the words: "So shall it be done!"

Hoofbeats sounded then, and I knelt clutching my tree as the noise of the Hunt echoed around me and receded into the distance, then at last faded away completely. I was alone only for a minute, though. I heard a happy bark and then felt Ove licking my cheeks, which were wet already with tears of worry and fear that I had not known I'd shed. I tore off my blindfold and threw my arms around the dog, whose tail wagged so violently that it nearly threw him to the ground. The nisse was with him, and he gave me a nod.

"Not badly done," he said grudgingly, and I smiled through my tears at his idea of a compliment. I looked around quickly; the cloak clasp was nowhere in sight, and there was no sign of either Hunt or elves. Then I noticed a movement amid the trees and stood to see what approached.

"Oh, look," I said softly.

Through the trees marched a line of children, with

Kai at their head. Some were tiny, some merely little; none was older than six or seven. There were dozens of them. Some of the older and larger ones carried infants in their arms. They looked healthy enough, well fed, and most were blinking and rubbing their eyes as if they had been long asleep. Ove gave a great bark, and the children broke ranks then, chattering and crowding around the dog to pet him. Kai bent to give Ove a hug and then straightened, his eyes finding mine across the children's bowed heads.

"Lilia!" he exclaimed. "What has happened? Where are we?" He was so full of questions that he had to stop speaking entirely. I made my way to him and threw my arms around him. His own strong arms pulled me tightly to him. I could hardly speak for joy.

"Oh, Kai," I breathed. "I have missed you so! I'm sorry it took so long. We had to get to the palace, and—oh! And I am a princess! And Karina—she loves the prince—"

"What?" Kai said, beginning to laugh and releasing me. "What are you talking about? You—a princess? Karina—in love? How long have I been in this cursed place?"

"Many days," I told him, and the laughter faded from his face.

"So long? It feels like almost no time has passed

since I walked up to the feast!" he said incredulously. "I remember a bonfire, a great deal of food . . . that is all."

"That was at Midsummer," I said. "It has been nearly a fortnight since then."

"It's elf-magic that makes the time all funny," the nisse said, and Kai stared at him.

"Why, it's our own nisse from the farm!" he exclaimed.

"He has been such a help to us," I said.

The nisse looked rather pleased, an unfamiliar expression on his sour face; and he bowed his head to me, very slightly.

"Just doing my job, Your Highness," he said modestly. "Though rather better than most, I'll wager."

"Is it true, then?" Kai asked. "Are you really a princess?"

"I suppose I am," I replied. "I've not had much time to get used to it, though."

"How can all that have happened when it seems that no time has passed? I have been lost in a dream," Kai said, bewildered. Then he gazed at the children who stood around us. "But these children—how long have they been in the dream?"

"Look at their clothes," I said to him, pointing out what I had noticed when I first saw the captives serving at the Midsummer's Eve feast. "Some of them are dressed in garments from years and years ago. How many of them are decades, even centuries old?"

Their sweet faces looked up at us. None of them appeared even as old as ten, yet some must have been hundreds of years old. "We must get them out of the forest, and find their families," I said. "Nisse, will you guide us?"

The nisse frowned. "Do you think I've nothing better to do?"

I was learning how to handle the nisse, so I replied, as sweetly as I imagined Karina might, "I know you have important work to see to, but we have great need of you."

The nisse rolled his eyes, but I imagined I could see some pleasure in his grizzled face. "I suppose I could take the time," he said offhandedly.

We gathered the children together and set out in a line. As we walked, I proceeded to fill Kai in on the astonishing things that had happened. I told of my bargain with the Elf-King, of how we had found employment at the palace, of the test of the hopeful brides, of the deepening love between Karina and the prince. I recounted how we had snuck into the locked chamber, how I had found the cloak clasp and passed the test. He was shocked when I explained the discovery that I was the princess of Dalir. When I described facing down Odin and trading the cloak clasp for the prisoners, he whistled and shook his head.

"Well, I suppose I know my worth now," he said wryly. "A cloak clasp for my life!"

I laughed. "It was a very special jewel," I pointed out. "And I am very glad that its value was greater than yours—to Odin, at any rate."

"Only to Odin?" he teased me. "Did you not value the clasp?"

I blushed. "Well, I traded it for you, did I not?"

"Does this mean that I am yours now?" Kai asked in a new tone, one that was gentle and warm.

"Oh," I said softly, not sure if he was still teasing. "Do you want to be?"

Kai reached out his free hand and took mine. "I can think of worse fates," he replied, and if I hadn't just then tripped over a root and almost dropped the baby I carried, I believe he might have stopped walking and kissed me.

12

A TRUE PRINCESS
WINS THE DAY

Kai and I trudged along the endless path that I had taken before with Karina, only now we had dozens of hungry, tired, frightened, confused children to tend as well. "Where are we going?" they asked, and "When will we get there?" The nisse was annoyed almost to desperation by their complaints, and disappeared often to smoke his pipe. He would return in a state of near calm that lasted only until the next "My feet hurt!" or "I'm starving!" Kai and I tried to carry the littlest ones and encourage the rest, but I was stumbling with exhaustion, and even Kai and Ove were plodding along quite grimly when the trees at last began to thin.

"We're almost there," I whispered to Kai. I held a child in one arm, but he took my free hand again and squeezed it. Hand in hand thus, we reached the edge of the trees. I had no idea how long I had been gone, for as the nisse had said, time was a strangely flexible thing in the realm of the Elf-King. I'd hoped it was only days, not weeks or months—or years—and that the encampment, with my parents, Karina, and the knights, would still be waiting for us. But never did I expect what I saw in the meadow outside the gloom of Bitra Forest.

I blinked, squinting in the sudden sunshine, and tried to make sense of it. Many more tents were spread across the field, some ornate and decorated as the royal tents were, some makeshift affairs that looked as if a strong wind would carry them away. There were cook-fires everywhere, children playing between the tents, people moving to and fro carrying buckets of water, sacks of foodstuffs, items too varied to be named. An entire town was there, it seemed—all of Gilsa, moved from its stone houses to tents in a field. Openmouthed, I stopped and stared, and when I turned to Kai I could see the same shock on his face that I felt.

Then a woman, gray haired but with a lively face and manner, spotted us. Her arms held a pile of clothes that fell unnoticed into the dirt. Her hands flew to her rosy cheeks and the blood drained from them, and for a moment I thought she too would collapse onto the ground. Instead she cried out wordlessly, and then she wailed, "My Peder! My baby, Peder! Oh look, it is my baby, come back to me!"

A boy of four or five years darted out of the woods and ran to the woman. He leaped into her arms with such force that she tumbled backward, landing with a *thump* atop her laundry. Other family members hurried over to the pair, and there was a great uproar and a tangle of arms and legs, hugs and kisses.

Mothers and fathers, grandparents, and other kinfolk of those stolen scores of years before came from the tents and held open their arms. Their lost children rushed forward and into their waiting embraces, somehow knowing just where they belonged. Though the changelings had stayed children, their families had aged, so there were young married folk welcoming their three-year-old great-aunts and aged crones hugging their infant brothers. The scene was chaos, tumult, and delight, and I thrilled to see the joyful reunions of families who thought they would never again see their loved ones. All the children found their families, until only Kai, the nisse, and I stood at the forest's edge.

The crowd parted suddenly, and there were the

king and queen, Tycho and Karina moving toward us. Karina burst into tears and ran ahead, throwing herself into Kai's arms. They hugged, and then she hugged me, and then she hugged Kai again, weeping all the while. Finally I had to say to her, "You must stop crying! Else your nose will turn all red and drip, and the prince will not like you anymore." That made her laugh, and she tried to dry her eyes with her sleeve. Then she noticed the nisse.

"Why, it's you!" she said to him. "Have you helped us again, you dear creature?"

I would never have thought a nisse could blush, but blush he did. He ducked his head and scuffed his foot on the ground as I related his deeds, and Karina put her arms around him. He stood stock-still, his weathered face as red as his cap, and mumbled, "Lady, you are unseemly! Let me go!"

"In a minute," Karina said. She bent and kissed his cheek and then released him. The nisse raised his hand to his cheek, his mouth a round O of surprise. Then he spun on his heel and rushed back into the forest, disappearing before I could call him back; and I laughed until tears came to my eyes at the expression on his face, a combination of bliss and utter embarrassment.

The king and queen and prince stood patiently

waiting as finally we turned our backs on Bitra Forest for good. My mother's embrace was like balm to me, and Tycho's hug came with a whisper: "Karina has said yes!" that made me squeeze him with joy. But when my father put his arms around me, I yielded to a sudden exhaustion so deep that I feared I might faint again. The king lifted me in his arms and said, "Daughter, you have done well. Now you must rest."

After that all was hazy to me. I know we went straight to the palace and I was put in the softest, most luxurious bed imaginable. There were no lumps, no bumps, no pea hidden beneath the mattress to disturb my slumber. I slept a deep and dreamless sleep and woke refreshed to find Karina at the dressing table near my bed, experimenting with her hair. Ove was curled on an embroidered pillow in a corner, and he wagged his tail when he noticed that my eyes were open.

"Good morning," I said groggily.

"Good afternoon!" Karina replied, turning and smiling at me. "I have a tray here with some food for you; you must be half starved. You've slept a very long time!"

"I may never get up," I said lazily, stretching with pleasure. I reached for the tray of cheeses and bread, breaking off pieces to toss to Ove, who could not jump up high enough to reach my lofty mattress.

"Oh, but you must get up!" Karina said. "The whole town is having a party tonight, and it is all for you. You are like a hero in a legend, Lilia! They are composing songs in your honor!"

"Oh my," I said wonderingly. "Songs? Really?" I was quite pleased, to tell the truth. Then I recalled something that had happened just before I was overcome by exhaustion. "Karina," I said, "did Tycho tell me—did he say that you had consented to his proposal? Have you agreed to marry my brother?"

"I have," she admitted shyly. "While you were gone, we came to an understanding. He spoke with the king and queen, and they have accepted me, though I am not of royal blood. They say that if you and I are as sisters, and if their son loves me, then I am their daughter already."

"Then tonight we must celebrate your engagement as well!" I cried, and I climbed out of bed. "What shall we wear? How shall we do our hair?" I went to the closet, and there I found dresses in every color and fabric, in sizes to fit both Karina and myself.

"Is this magic?" I asked in astonishment. "Where did these come from?"

"Your mother had them made while we waited for you to come out of the forest," Karina told me.

"What?" I said, confused. "How long was I gone?"

"A fortnight and a day," Karina answered. "You didn't know?"

"I had no idea," I confessed. "It could have been a day, or a week, or a year. There is no way to tell in that cursed forest. That explains how so many had gathered by the time we returned, though."

"The people came from Gilsa gradually," Karina explained. "As the story spread that you had gone to get the changelings, their families began to make their way to us. It was wondrous, to see them come. Old and young they came, so full of hope and love for their lost children—and you brought their babies back, Lilia! Oh, I am so proud of you!" She embraced me, and I hugged her in return.

"But tell me," I said, remembering something else. "The falcons—did you know they saved me? Where did they come from?" I told her how the falcons had swooped down and taken the elves' arrows from them, and her eyes grew very wide at the thought of the danger I'd been in.

"That was Sir Erlend's doing," she said. "I don't know what made him think of it; but that first day after you disappeared into the wood, he went up to the mews, and he let the falcons out. Everyone thought they were gone for good, but then the birds came back, each carrying a quiver of elvish arrows. Your mother almost collapsed. Her fear for you was great, but we had no way to find out what had happened or where you were. And now we know that Sir Erlend's idea worked!"

"Indeed, I must thank him," I said. "I believe his cleverness saved my life."

Then we chose our dresses. I wore lavender satin, and Karina decided on blue silk. She interlaced strands of her blond hair with pearls, leaving the rest to fall in golden curls down her back. Her bright blue eyes matched the sapphire of her dress.

"Are you sure you don't want to wear a braid?" I teased her, and she slapped at me, hitting only air as I dodged away.

"As long as I don't have to fear setting my hair ablaze in the cookfire, I will never again wear a braid," she said decisively.

"Nor I," I agreed, sitting before the looking glass. Karina fixed my hair, weaving it through with amethysts, and then we admired our reflections. "You look beautiful," I told Karina, and she said, "No, *you* look beautiful, Your Highness!"

"You are Your Highness as well, you know," I pointed out.

"Not yet," she said decisively. "I will be plain Karina until Midwinter, when we wed."

But she was not plain Karina, for my father made

Kai a knight and Karina a lady that afternoon before we went down to the town. She was Lady Karina then, and Kai was Sir Kai, though I teased him mercilessly for it.

"You look every inch the lord, Sir Kai," I told him afterward, taking in his well-groomed curls, his velvet doublet and scrubbed hands.

"Nothing in my life has prepared me for this!" he admitted, laughing. "I sometimes think I will wake up to find myself on the hillside in Hagi, tending my sheep."

"Do you miss the farm?" I asked him.

"I miss Papa," he said a little sadly. "But you know that I always dreaded the thought of spending my life among the sheep, though I never said so to him. I didn't think there was any other path open to me."

"Well," I said, "we must bring your father here for the wedding, then."

"But what of Ylva?" he asked.

"The wedding will be at the winter solstice, and she will have had the baby not long before," I pointed out. "She will not come."

Kai smiled. "It would make Karina tremendously happy to have Papa there," he told me. "She said that she would not invite him, for she did not want you ever to have to face Ylva again, but I know it saddened her."

"Jorgen should walk her down the aisle," I agreed.

"Oh, imagine Papa walking down the aisle in a royal chapel, in his farm clothes and his great beard!"

"And smoking his pipe," I added mischievously. "I think we can find him a new suit of clothes for the occasion, though."

We laughed, and then together with the king and queen, and Tycho and Karina, with Ove frolicking behind, we set out on foot down the hill to Gilsa.

In the great town square an enormous bonfire had been lit, and the townspeople crowded around it. There were many toasts to Prince Tycho and Karina, and Karina was thrilled to see that all the town seemed happy about the engagement. Families came to me with their thanks, and I kissed the children I had rescued, glad to see them with their loved ones. I listened to the minstrels singing about my adventures. Most of their songs were very bad indeed, though there was one verse I rather liked:

"So Princess Lilia all in danger stood
And faced the Elf-King with his sword and shield,
And working only for her people's good
She did not flinch, nor ever did she yield."

The crowd learned it quickly and sang it loudly, shouting the last line, and I laughed. Of course it was ridiculous, for the Elf-King had no sword or shield, and I did indeed flinch many times. But I liked it nonetheless, and I hummed its tune as I danced with the people of Gilsa. Even the king and queen danced among their subjects.

Kai found me warming my hands by the bonfire as the evening began to draw to a close.

"I have been watching you tonight, you know," he told me.

"Watching me?" I looked at him quizzically.

"Yes, watching you undergo this . . . transformation. Becoming a princess. But I think it is not really such an alteration."

"No?" I asked, fascinated.

Kai smiled and said, "Oh, your clothes are different, and your hair—I do miss that braid! But the rest of it—your manners, your bearing, all that—it just seems to me like a . . . a sharpening."

"What do you mean?"

"I am saying this badly, I know. I mean that all the elements were already there. You were a bad servant to Ylva because you were a princess. You were always a true princess, even when you were a shepherdess. I can see that now." He stopped talking, a little flustered, and I mulled over his words.

"I don't know if that's true," I said finally, "but it's a wonderful excuse for my shortcomings as a serving maid. I doubt that it would convince Ylva, though!"

We laughed, and then I asked seriously, "Does that mean you think I will not change much, being a princess?"

Kai looked thoughtful. "You do not seem quite the sleepless maiden you once were. I'm glad of that—I don't have to worry about you dozing off in the middle of a conversation anymore. And you are already more sure of yourself, less uncertain. And yet—" He broke off.

"And yet what?" I asked, raising my face to his.

"And yet, to me you will always be the Lilia who breaks the plates and cooks lumpy porridge," he said, grinning; and at last he kissed me.

Then we joined Karina and Tycho, and the four of us danced until the moon set and the edges of the sky began to lighten. Exhausted and happy, we made our way back up the hill to the palace with Ove now trailing bedraggled behind us; the king and queen had long before gone up to bed.

"Oh, my poor feet!" I groaned, not used to the heels I had worn that night. I longed for my lovely mattress and a deep, deep sleep.

"But it was wonderful," Karina said, taking my hand and pulling me up the steep cobblestones. "It is all too wonderful to be real. It seems like a dream."

I turned and looked down at the town spread out

below us, my town in my own kingdom, where the bonfire still smoldered and the reunited families slept, cozy in their stone houses. Then I looked up at the palace perched atop the hill, where I would get to know my parents and learn to be a princess, where Tycho and Karina would be married.

"No," I said softly to Karina, and to Tycho and Kai, shaking my head. "It is not a dream. My life before this was the dream. This—this is the awakening."